THE WOLF AT NUMBER 4

MODERN
African
Writing
from Ohio University Press

Laura T. Murphy and Ainehi Edoro, Series Editors

This series brings the best African writing to an international audience. These groundbreaking novels, memoirs, and other literary works showcase the most talented writers of the African continent. The series also features works of significant historical and literary value translated into English for the first time. Moderately priced, the books chosen for the series are well crafted, original, and ideally suited for African studies classes, world literature classes, or any reader looking for compelling voices of diverse African perspectives.

The Wolf at Number 4

A NOVEL

Ayo Tamakloe-Garr

OHIO UNIVERSITY PRESS • ATHENS

Ohio University Press, Athens, Ohio 45701
ohioswallow.com
© 2018 by Ayo Tamakloe-Garr

To obtain permission to quote, reprint, or otherwise reproduce or distribute
material from Ohio University Press publications, please contact our rights
and permissions department at (740) 593-1154 or (740) 593-4536 (fax).

Printed in the United States of America
Ohio University Press books are printed
on acid-free paper ⊗ ™

28 27 26 25 24 23 22 21 20 19 18   5 4 3 2 1

Library of Congress Cataloging-in-Publication Data
Names: Tamakloe-Garr, Ayo, 1992- author.
Title: The wolf at number 4 : a novel / Ayo Tamakloe-Garr.
Other titles: Wolf at number four
Description: Athens : Ohio University Press, 2018. | Series: Modern african
    writing series
Identifiers: LCCN 2018038480| ISBN 9780821423547 (hardback) | ISBN
    9780821423554 (pb) | ISBN 9780821446584 (pdf)
Subjects: | BISAC: FICTION / General. | LITERARY COLLECTIONS / African.
Classification: LCC PR9379.9.T36 W65 2018 | DDC 823/.92--dc23
LC record available at https://lccn.loc.gov/2018038480

For T

and

For K.

I appreciate it all. I really do

prologue

MAYBE ALL THIS HAPPENED BECAUSE MR. ADDISON tried to rape me. For a man old enough to be my father, he sure was strong.

Mike would have slapped his palm against his forehead if he had found out. Then he would have hugged me or something, and then after, gone to break Mr. Addison's jaw. Mike was wonderful like that. When I asked him what he saw in Hannah, he said she was "some woman." Noticing my expression, he added, "You've always been more person to me." Half an hour later he married Hannah in the suit I had bought for him.

So maybe it was Hannah after all.

A cold gust brings me out of my thoughts. I am cold and numb. My throat is dry and cries out for something warm and sweet and comforting. Uncle Johnny gave me my first taste of wine when I was fourteen. I remember that night so vividly.

Maybe it was Uncle Johnny, rather.

I bite back the tears welling up behind my eyes. Kind of the way Augustine had attempted to. Augustine had not been one of my best decisions. I hadn't told Wolf this, but Augustine had sort of gone off the rails afterwards. I had not been good for Augustine.

Wolf—maybe it was him.

Or maybe his father or his mother?

Or Nii?

Or was it the cancer that took my father?

Or the miscarriage?

Maybe it was Junior.

Maybe it was Jeff being so self-absorbed.

Maybe it was the Fire-Eater's animosity towards me.

Or maybe, maybe it was me.

Maybe all this happened because I was *me*. But then could I be anything else?

I shake my head. I'm beginning to sound like Wolf already.

Another chilly breeze hits me.

"Ɔdɔ!" calls the young dreadlocked man in the BMW to my left. He licks his lips. His invitation hangs in the air like a disembodied hand, caressing my chin and beckoning me towards warmth.

I look around the filling station in the middle of nowhere. I have to find somewhere to go soon, but everywhere—Cape Coast, Accra—is the deep blue sea. And the sea has proven to be anything but warm.

The devil is still looking at me, *all* of the me he can see.

I wrap my arms around myself. Boy, is it cold out here.

Boy, am I cold.

1

MR. ADDISON SEEMED GENUINELY NICE WHEN HE hired me five minutes into my interview, not even asking what happened with my old job in Accra.

When I told him about my mother and I having to relocate to a dingy compound house after my father died, he gave me a cosy little colonial era bungalow to live in. He then suggested a fun trip to the Grand Cape resort in Elmina that Saturday night, after I had moved in.

And it was fun at first.

Then came the touchiness—holding my hand, wrapping another round my waist, then "playfully" smacking my rear. Nevertheless, I followed him up to the hotel room. Maybe I wanted to believe that he would turn out different, that Cape Coast would be different, a fresh start. Anyway, what saved me was his heart giving up on him.

In the emergency room after the heart attack, the nurses rushed past, and each one of them gave me the eyes. It was not hard to know what they were thinking. He was married and old and rich. I was unmarried and young and my dress was high above my knees.

What the nurses thought, Mr. Addison's driver said. When he dropped me off at the junction leading into West End Ridge, he muttered "Ashawo" before slamming the door and speeding off.

My house, number 3, sat atop the ridge and was the farthest from the main road. But fortunately, West End Ridge was a small neighborhood with the houses far apart and surrounded by trees and shrubs. I hadn't seen a single neighbor since I moved in the day before, and I was glad no one was around to see my puffy eyes and the bright red stain on the white, polka-dotted dress I was wearing.

I had met many Mr. Addisons; I just never learned. The doctors said this latest one would be fine but he would have to live life at a much slower pace. Not that I cared anyway. I just wanted to fall into bed and wash the previous night's events from my memory.

But it was then that I met my first neighbor.

The bungalows in West End Ridge all had the same basic format. Two bedrooms, a bathroom, kitchen, and living room. The back door opened into a garage, and the front door opened into a porch bounded by a low wall and a small wooden gate. Well, perched on my porch wall was a little boy.

He looked no more than ten or eleven, and he sat perfectly still. I dragged my feet to get his attention, but he kept on staring off into the distance. Even as I unlocked the porch gate, he just sat there, unmoving.

"Hello," I called out.

There was no response.

I took cautious steps towards him. Nothing.

He only reacted when I tapped him on the shoulder. His thick, bushy eyebrows slanted down towards each other, and his large, bulging, owl-like eyes fixed themselves intently on me.

"'Nevermore,'" he whispered.

"What?"

"'Thus quoth the raven.'"

"What?"

"Never mind," he said. He hopped off the short porch wall and into the grass. "I don't think you're coming from church."

I folded my arms. "No, I'm not."

"I saw you yesterday. You went out with Mr. Addison. Is this your house?"

"Yes it is," I replied. "Who are you? What is your name?"

"My name is Wolfgang. But you should call me Wolf. It's shorter. And . . . " He paused and mischief crept onto his face. "Do you want me to tell you a secret?"

My curiosity got the better of my desire to just fall into my bed, so I nodded.

He beckoned me closer and whispered into my ear. "I may look like one, but I'm not a human. I'm a wolf."

I laughed and he set his jaw and balled his fists.

"Look, little boy," I said to him. "Where do you live?"

He pointed behind me. I turned to look.

"Number 4. That's my house."

"I see. Well, you can't just come sit on someone else's wall like that. People don't do that. It's an invasion of my privacy. Do you understand?"

He nodded.

"Good boy."

"I'm going home," he announced. He started to walk away but turned back to me and said, "Edgar Allan Poe. You should read more."

I couldn't help making a face. "I probably read 'The Raven' before you were born."

He stopped. "Then you may be of some use to me," he said. "Maybe." And then he continued on his way.

I kissed my teeth and went inside. I immediately stepped out of my dress and took it to the sink. The dress was a gift from a dear old friend. In his attempt to get at me, Mr. Addison had knocked over a bottle of Merlot that I had ordered. Having had the entire night to set and dry, the stain refused to come out. So I threw the dress onto one of the unpacked suitcases that lay strewn about my living room.

I contemplated calling my mother, but I couldn't bear to hear the disappointment in her voice when she found out that I had blown yet another, and possibly my last, chance. She worried about me far more than was healthy for someone with a blood pressure of 160 over 100.

When prostate cancer took my father, we lost everything. We lost the houses and the cars. I lost my opportunity to get my master's degree and eventually even my job.

That night, as I waited for sleep to arrive, I wondered if I should have just let Addison have his way. I wondered if I was too naïve and too soft for this world. Father had always said so, never in a harsh manner, but when I look back now, with a sort of remorse. Perhaps he knew how I was to end up. Father always knew.

I got up, dug into one of my suitcases, pulled out a bottle of red wine, downed a glass or two, and returned to my bed.

2

THE TEN-MINUTE WALK FROM MY HOUSE TO Lighthouse Academy would have been pleasant on any other day. It was a slow descent into a valley and up a gentle slope to the crest of another ridge. The road was shaded by tall and ancient-looking trees. In places, their canopies had merged to form arches. But as I walked through the chilly dawn air, only thoughts of my imminent sacking occupied my mind. Addison was going to have it done, if he couldn't do it himself.

The reporting time was at seven o'clock, but I was there at half past six. Mr. Addison had already given me a tour, so I knew where the staff common room was and which wooden table and chair was mine. I set my water bottle down on the desk and took a seat. I started to flip through the syllabus while I waited for the other teachers to show up. The first one arrived fifteen minutes past eight.

"Wow!" he exclaimed the moment he walked in. He was tall and reasonably good looking. He had his first button opened and his cuffs folded upwards. Unfortunately, he reeked of cockiness.

I gave him a wave and a smile.

He approached my desk and extended his hand. "You must be the new English teacher."

I rose and took his hand. "Yes, I am. My name is Desire Mensah."

"I'm Gerald Amponsah. But you call me Gerald, okay. You're very pretty."

"Thank you, Gerald. It's nice to meet you," I said, and sat.

"It's my pleasure," he said licking his lips. "Desire ampa."

I smiled with my lips only and looked down at my books.

But he sat on the edge of my desk and crossed his legs. "So, you're from Accra, I hear." He opened his bag and brought out a sachet of yogurt, bit the edge off, spat it out onto the floor, and proceeded to drink. Beads of condensed water dropped on my desk and books.

"Yes, I am," I said, slowly.

"And you were a teacher there?"

"Yes, I taught at Cantonments International School."

"Wow! CIS paah. So why did you leave?" He was chewing noisily on the frozen yogurt through the sachet now.

"The school board and I didn't see eye to eye on certain issues."

"What issues?"

I almost sighed out loud.

Fortunately, the door opened and in walked two people. One was a lanky, stern-looking man and the other an even sterner-looking woman. I recognized the man from my interview; he was the HR. The woman was new to me. She looked masculine, with her natural hair shaved low, square shoulders, and severe expression. I wondered if these were my executioners.

"Mr. Gyamfi!" exclaimed Gerald, jumping up off my desk and wiping his wet palms on his trousers. "Good morning."

Mr. Gyamfi's eyes roamed about the room. "Morning, Gerald. The others are not in?"

"No, sir. It's just me, sir. Me and Miss Mensah."

Mr. Gyamfi's gaze fixed itself on me. "Ah, Miss Mensah. How are you settling in?"

I stepped forward and shook his hand. "Just fine, sir." I nodded in the direction of the woman, but her hard and set expression remained unchanged.

"Good," he said. "Anyway, Mr. Addison unfortunately suffered a heart attack on Saturday night, if you haven't heard already."

Gerald covered his mouth. "Ow!"

My heart started to pound through my ears.

"Yes, it's unfortunate. So he has to go on immediate retirement. It's overdue anyway." He turned to the woman beside him. "So the school board has selected Mrs. Providencia Anaglate here to take over as headmistress."

The woman nodded.

"You're welcome, madam," said Gerald, shaking her hand.

The disdain in the woman's eyes was evident as she observed Gerald from behind her bifocals. After a moment, she said, "Thank you." She then glanced at her wristwatch. "It's half past eight, right?"

"Yes, it is, madam," said Gerald, oblivious to what she actually meant.

Providencia Anaglate then made it clear to him. "We'll fix the tardiness. Anyway, that will be all for now. Nice to meet you, Mr. Gerald, and welcome, Miss Mensah." I was too nervous to speak, so I just shook her hand as well. Her grip was firm. "I hope you enjoy working here."

I mumbled my thanks as they left the room.

Gerald turned to me and started to talk, but I didn't hear a thing he said. The relief was incredible. I found myself grinning.

" . . . it happens to you too, eh?" Gerald said, and laughed.

He hadn't noticed my mind was elsewhere. My grin turned into laughter, and I nodded in agreement to whatever he had said.

"Can I drink some of your water?" he asked, his eyes on my water bottle.

I smiled and shook my head.

The other teachers arrived not too long after that, and the news of Mr. Addison's heart attack spread through the common room like wildfire.

After one teacher asked what happened, Mr. Baiden, the RME teacher, got up with a roguish look on his face and said, "Hmm, mmaasɛm oh. You know Papa Addison already."

Everyone erupted in raucous laughter. Everyone except me. I just tried to look amused.

Baiden continued, "I heard he was at the resort with a woman, some fine woman bi like that."

"Ei Baiden," cried someone.

"Oh true thing I de talk," he protested. "They said eh . . . " He then lowered his voice after glancing around. "They said Papa Addison and the girl went to chill and he spread the girl fine fine. And when they went inside for the dessert, then he had the heart attack."

The ensuing laughter was even louder than the first. "Ei Baiden!" someone exclaimed.

"He couldn't handle it, eh?" came Gerald.

Baiden returned to his seat. "E no be easy koraa." He then pretended to zip his lips. "But me I didn't say anything oh."

I pretended to laugh along with everyone, although I was horrified at how much they knew.

Fortunately, the topic switched to Providencia Anaglate. Baiden apparently had a friend whose brother-in-law's cousin had worked with someone who taught under her at her previous school. And according to that person, she did not play around at all. They called her Madam Fire-Eater. They said when she discovered her husband in bed with a level 100 girl, she whipped the two of them with a belt and sent her husband howling down the street naked.

At the moment, I didn't care about her. I didn't even care that Gerald had perched himself on my desk again. I was just glad I had my job and that my identity as the mystery woman from that infamous night remained secret.

3

MY WALK HOME TOOK ME THROUGH THE PRIMARY section of the school. Consisting of six classes as opposed to three forms, it was obviously much bigger than the JSS section. But it wasn't just the size that caught my attention. Both the lower and upper primary blocks were nicely painted. They were beige with brown strips around their base. The administration block, a gleaming white two-story building, had sliding glass windows, and the air conditioners behind the block whirred away in the afternoon heat. In front of the block was a magnificent statue of a child gazing off into the distance with a book in hand. The lawns around all the blocks were actual lawns. They were neatly kept carpets of luxurious green grass, not the dirty brown patches of weeds we had at the JSS section.

Although it was an hour after their closing time, there were still quite a number of pupils about, chasing each other up and down corridors and playing in the grass or the jungle gym or seesaws and slides.

Under an old mango tree near the wire fence which marked the edge of the school compound, about twenty children were standing in four columns. They seemed to be reciting something while a solitary kid paced in front of them. I assumed they were playing, perhaps reenacting a classroom scene.

As I drew closer to them, I realized the child in front was no other than that weird kid I had found on my porch. On cue from him, the others raised their arm to shoulder level with their palms and hands straight out. Then they all began to chant, "Heil der Wolf!"

The salute must have been the end of their meeting, for they began to disperse. By the time I arrived at the mango tree, only the brat stood proudly in his spot.

"Herh! What was that?" I asked him, hands on hips.

"An assembly of my little sheep," he replied with a smile. "We do this at the beginning of every week to reaffirm their commitment to the cause."

"What cause?"

"My cause. They are my sheep."

"So what are you supposed to be, some tyrant or dictator or what?

He laughed. "You say it like it's a bad thing."

"Really?"

"It's not my fault I have the power," he said with a shrug.

My hands went back onto my hips.

He looked into my eyes. "Stop giving me that look. Are the sheep innocent just because they don't have claws and sharp teeth?"

I shook my head. "You're unbelievable. There really is something wrong with you." I started to walk away.

He ran after me. "If it makes any difference, it was originally a Roman salute, you know."

"I don't care."

He was alongside me now. "It used to be a Roman salute. There's no reason to be upset."

I didn't respond.

He walked beside me in silence for a while. Then he said, "You don't like me much, do you?"

Of course I didn't. But it was hard to tell that straight to a kid's face. I sighed. "You did a bad thing."

He looked down at the ground. "It's okay. A lone wolf doesn't have friends anyway."

"What about your friends back there?"

He laughed. "Friends? They are nothing more than sheep. I care nothing for them. They fear me because I manipulate and bully them. I call them my sheep and they hail me as their wolf leader. How dumb can they be?"

"And you're happy saying that?"

"It's just the truth. But I can dissolve the group if you want. It's an experiment that has run its course."

"Why do you care what I want?"

"You're not a sheep. I can tell."

"Really?"

He nodded. "You haven't told me your name."

"Desire."

"Desire?" he repeated. "That's an odd name."

"It's not any odder than yours. Which Ghanaian is called Wolfgang?"

"Wolf," he said, jumping over a pothole. "My father likes Mozart. Mozart's first name was—"

"I know."

"Sorry," he said. "I've dealt with sheep too long."

I smiled against my will. "Don't worry," I said, suppressing the smile. "I don't know why I was called Desire, unfortunately."

He jumped over another pothole. "Ask your father, then."

"My father is dead."

"Too bad," he said. "My mother, my real mother, is dead too."

"Oh, I'm sorry."

He shrugged. "I didn't know her."

A truck appeared from behind us. We moved over to one side of the road and watched it slowly navigate the potholes. It was a dark blue color, and in the back faces squashed themselves against a wire mesh. Some of the faces watched us with curiosity. And some faces glared at us as if we were the reason they were in the back of the truck.

Then a hand squeezed itself through the mesh and opened in our direction.

Wolfgang ran up to the truck, reaching into his schoolbag.

"Herh!" I cried.

The boy pulled out his food flask and offered it to the hand, which grabbed hold of the flask by the handle. Several more hands appeared through the mesh and gasped at the flask. The truck disappeared around the bend with the hands holding the flask against the mesh.

"Why did you do that?" I asked him. "Don't you know they are thieves and murderers and rapists?"

He shrugged. "It's boiled yam and kontonmire. I hate that stuff."

We started walking again. "Your mother is going to kill you when she finds out the flask is gone," I told him.

"She wouldn't dare," he said. "No one can touch me."

He then ran ahead to the fork that split the road into two, one leading to my house and the other to his.

"Come!" he cried and gestured. "Come to my house and meet my daddy."

Number 4, West End Ridge sat about a hundred meters opposite my house. Although the bungalows were identical in every way, this one looked considerably older than mine. The asphalt path leading up to it was weathered and potholed. The large wooden garage door had started to rot at its base, and black fungi ran down its walls, looking like mascara tears.

In the driveway was a gray pickup truck. A big and imposing man I presumed to be his father walked around it, inspecting the wheels. He moved with the authority of a person who was aware he could beat any obstacle into submission. I felt small and awkward as I approached him.

"Good afternoon," I said.

He turned around. "Afternoon." His voice was as authoritative as his manner, and his eyes regarded me suspiciously.

"She's a new teacher at my school, Daddy," explained Wolfgang. "She teaches JSS."

His father shot him a look that scared even me. "No one asked you, young man. Go inside and study."

"Goodbye, Desire," he said, and waved. "See you tomorrow."

"Desire, eh?" asked his father.

"Yes. Desire Mensah. I teach at your son's school like he said."

He took my hand and shook it. "Stanley Ofori. I'm a lecturer at the university."

"That's impressive. What do you teach?"

"Metamorphic petrology. I'm a geologist." He pointed to boxes in his pickup. "I'm just returning from the field, as you can see. Those are my samples."

"That's interesting. Can I take a look?"

He pulled out a pocket knife and cut the tape sealing one box. Inside were small, roughly fist-sized rocks. Most were dark colored, almost black. But one caught my eye. I picked it up to take a closer look. It had black and white stripes and red spots scattered all over it.

"I had always thought of rocks as hard, dirty brown things," I said. "So what will you do with them?"

"Many things, petrographic studies, chemical analysis. But these are things you shouldn't worry your head with." He took back the rock and threw it back in the box. He then yelled "Junior!" so loud I jumped.

A man roughly my age emerged. "Yes, Da."

"Come and pack these things inside."

He obliged. I stepped backwards to give him way.

"This is our neighbor, Mrs. Mensah, by the way," his father said.

"Miss," I corrected.

Junior nodded at me. "Nice to meet you."

"You too," I replied, but he had already turned away.

"That's my firstborn," Mr. Ofori said.

"Oh."

"So why aren't you married?" he asked me.

"Well . . . "

"Don't tell me you are one of those so-called feminists," he growled. "You don't believe in marriage, eh? You don't want to submit yourself to a man?"

"No, I just—"

"Let me tell you something. I know women like you. You be there and be following these white people blindly. Those people don't have any culture. You'll die alone. Nobody will marry you oh. Yoo."

"Oh, I have nothing against—"

"You this young generation, abandoning your culture for these sick Western ideas. Look at their societies, look at their divorce rates. Go and find a man and be a wife. No African man will tolerate this nonsense."

"Yes, sir."

"Good. Me, I've said my own. Goodbye, Miss Mensah."

He turned and left me there, feeling quite foolish and sorry for myself.

4

IN THE COMMON ROOM THE FOLLOWING DAY, I FOUND out why the primary school was in such a better state than the JSS.

"Have you heard of Wolfgang Ofori?" Baiden asked me.

"Yes. I've met him. He lives opposite my house sef. He's an odd child." I briefly considered telling them about the salute but decided against it.

"The boy is a genius," said Baiden.

"I noticed."

"The guy just wins quiz after quiz for the school. When you consider the grants and prize money he has won, it's like he has singlehandedly renovated the school. He's like the duck that lays golden eggs."

"As for me, I think that boy has an evil spirit," said Felicia, the social studies teacher.

"Hoh!" went Baiden.

Felicia turned in her seat to face us. "No, see, that child is very strange. He's not normal."

I frowned. "I think he's just playing most times. He is a child, after all."

"Why, you have also seen some of his things, eh?"

"Well, yes," I replied slowly. "He was playing with some of his mates."

"Aha! Did you see how much control he has over them? They fear him. You know what me I do? I never touch him in any of my classes. I pray before I even enter. Me deɛ, I like my life."

"Don't mind Felicia," Baiden told me.

"You don't know that some of these children are witches, eh?"

"And wizards."

"Whatever," she said. "It's all the same."

"Aren't you even a Christian, Felicia? What are you afraid of?" Baiden asked her.

She shook her head, turned back to her desk and muttered, "Yoo. Me deɛ, I've told you."

Baiden chuckled and said to me, "Have you heard of *Wonderkids*?"

I nodded. I watched it all the time back in Accra. It was a quiz program for senior secondary students. They were tested in six rounds on science, mathematics, history, English, critical reasoning, and general knowledge. It was a two-way knockout from the round of sixteen to the finals. The winners would get prestige and a large sum of money as spoil. However, if they could get a perfect score of 30,000 points, the prize was a hundred percent scholarship to an Ivy League school and a place in history for all three contestants. The highest anyone had gone was 23,500 points.

"Well, this year the Central Region will be hosting it, and our genius will be competing," said Baiden with a smile. "Think of the recognition it would bring the school."

"Ah. But he's just in primary school. How old is he?"

"Eleven. He's in class six. But honestly, the boy is good enough. They already agreed everything with his father. They'll register him for the BECE, and he'll write that and the SSCE as a private candidate."

"That's madness. It's too big a jump."

Baiden got up from his seat and asked me to come see something. He led me to the corner of the room, to where the file cabinets sat. He opened it and brought out a list. "This is the prize list for last year's speech and prize-giving day."

Every single prize that day had gone to Wolfgang.

Baiden handed me another list. "This is for the year before that."

It was the same. He had completed a clean sweep of all the awards.

"And it's the same going back to his first year here."

"This is incredible, but the jump is too big. The knowledge gap is just too wide."

Baiden closed the file cabinet. "His big brain can handle it. He knows everything he'd have to learn already. I mean he knows more than me saf. Besides, think of the history he could make, and the records he could break. His potential must be put to the greatest use. That's what his father said."

Gerald interrupted our conversation to tell me that Madam Fire-Eater wanted to see me.

The moment I stepped into Providencia Anaglate's office, my tummy began to feel hollow. She sat upright as ever at her neatly arranged desk. A large portrait of her rested on the wall behind her. It looked down at me contemptuously.

"You're welcome. Have a seat," she said, but I didn't feel welcome at all.

As she flipped through some papers on her desk, the harsh pencil-drawn eyes in the portrait burned into my soul.

"So," she eventually said. "There are a few things I'd like to clarify."

"Sure, madam. What is it?"

"The circumstances of your employment, Miss Mensah."

The hollow in my tummy grew a little. I shifted in my seat.

"What about it?"

She touched the bridge of her spectacles. "I can't find any documents relating to your interview. I've been going through Mr. Gyamfi's work for the last six months, and there's your job application and CV, but nothing about your interview."

"Mr. Gyamfi didn't interview me, madam," I said.

That caught her interest. "He didn't? Who did then?"

"Mr. Addison. I arrived on the eighteenth for the interview, and just as I was about to begin with Mr. Gyamfi, Mr. Addison said he would conduct it himself, so he took over."

She wrote something down. "I see."

"Okay then, Miss Mensah. I'll check Addison's documents and we'll sort this out. That will be all for now."

"Thank you, madam."

The hollow in my tummy didn't fade when I left her office. It stayed with me the entire day. I was keenly aware the bones of my past were not buried deeply enough. The moment the closing bell rang, I picked up my bag and left.

This time there was no herd of sheep under the mango tree. It was just Wolfgang. He was engrossed in a book which lay open on his lap.

"Hello, Wolfgang. How are you?" I asked him.

He sighed. "It's Wolf."

"Oh, sorry. What are you reading?"

He shut his book and rose, dusting off his shorts. "*Romeo and Juliet.*"

"Oh! I love it. It's such a beautiful and powerful story."

I remembered acting it out for the drama club all the way back in school. I was Juliet and tall and handsome Kojo was Romeo. He had such an enchanting smile and eyes that seemed to caress your soul every time he stared. Everyone said we worked well on stage. That was likely because he was my boyfriend off stage.

"I just finished it, and it's rubbish," said Wolf.

"What? *Romeo and Juliet*? How can you say that?"

He kicked a stone. "The writing is drawn out and tawdry at best. And the story is dumb. True love and all that? It's so corny and cliché. It makes my skin crawl."

I laughed. "I'm sure there's a lot you're glossing over. Don't you like the idea of true and pure love?"

He pretended to vomit. "Nothing is true and pure in this world. Human love is inherently selfish."

I laughed again. "One day you'll understand what love is."

"I certainly hope not!" he cried. Then he asked, "Are you in love?"

I shook my head. "No. My last relationship didn't go so well."

"That's not uncommon. What happened?"

I sighed. "He wanted too much from me. And too little at the same time. What about you? Have you ever had any crushes on your classmates?"

Something about that was incredibly hilarious to him. "No, no," he managed to say through his laughter. "Not at all. Although there was one girl with the potential to pique my interest, Korkor. She shared her kelewele with me in class two."

"That's nice."

"She's dead."

"Oh, that's terrible."

"We'll all die someday. And besides, she was human. I could never love a human."

He stopped walking and looked at me for a moment with mischief glowing in his eyes.

"Do you want to know what I will do when I grow up?" he asked.

"What?"

"I will drive the human race to extinction," he said with a grin.

"Herh! Why?"

"Think about it. I'd be doing every other organism on this earth a favor. Humans are the worst species to walk this planet. You know why? Because they are subjective. All I'm saying right now is being filtered and biased by your mind. How can you empathize if what you hear is not what I say? Humans are solitary animals because they cannot be objective. They all want to be 'the greatest sufferers.'" He paused for a moment. "How does that make you feel?"

I shrugged. "I don't know. But it certainly doesn't make me want to get rid of everyone. That sounds evil."

"Humans fight wars and hurt each other because they can't keep their subjectivity in check. We can't eliminate subjectivity. But we sure can eliminate humans. We wipe out humans, no wars and no evil and no pain. Simple."

"And so how do you think you're going to go about this?"

He touched his lip. "I've been thinking about that. Maybe I can do that through a world war. I'll need to rise to power, raise Ghana to a world superpower, become an evil dictator, start World War 3, and let nuclear fallout, disease, famine, and climate change do the rest."

"That sounds terrible."

"It's for the best. Or I could use an engineered supervirus. But that would require much biology, and biology is a lesser science. Or maybe an antimatter bomb of some sort would do." He was talking to himself now, and his voice faded into an undertone.

"I think it's going to be hard to tear all of this down," I said. "I think you'll meet some resistance."

He chuckled. "Hard? Even without me all this is going to end. You see, only some sort of divine intervention can save humanity from the precipice. Humans think they are so great, but civilization is really the greatest and most elaborate mass suicide the universe has ever seen. You humans, for all your flaws, have a wonderful eye for drama."

With every word he spoke, I felt a sadness grow within me. This was too much cynicism for an eleven-year-old.

"Tell me, Wolf," I said. "Do you want to be on the show? *Wonderkids?*"

"Why wouldn't I?"

"Are you sure?"

"I'd love it. It would be fun. And there's a nice scholarship waiting for me at the end."

I laid my hand on his shoulder and drew him closer to me. "To get the scholarship, though, you're going to have to jump the entirety of JSS and SSS, right?"

He lifted my arm off his shoulder. "I don't do physical contact. It's not behavior befitting a wolf."

"Oops. Sorry."

"Don't worry," he said. "You're just a human."

"So do you think you're ready?"

"Well, Daddy taped the show without the answers and made me go through the entire six rounds. And I scored 16,200 points."

I raised my eyebrows.

"And that was without any preparation or anything. So I should be able to reach the 30,000 score without too much trouble if I set my mind to it. In fact, one of the categories that let me down was English. Daddy says I read too many rubbish books about teenage space vampires."

"Oh really? Your English seems good. And didn't you even receive an award—"

"I told Daddy that you'll tutor me."

"Hmm ... "

"Would you?"

"I don't know. Frankly, I don't think I like the idea of you skipping so many years."

"I don't understand why it's a big deal."

"The gap will be just too far for you to bridge. It's impossible. Even if you have a good grasp of the academic work, you won't be able to handle the social changes. You won't be ready emotionally."

He scoffed at my last word. "I'm not prone to such afflictions. And 'impossible' is the word we use when we aren't determined enough. My brain has limitless potential. You have no reason to worry."

My words struggled on my lips. I remembered my own struggles with being jumped twice. Thirty minutes into my first paper at Legon, I broke down in tears. Apart from my name and index number, my answer sheet was blank. But it seemed almost criminal to tell a child that they couldn't do it all. So I just sighed.

He looked up at me and smiled. "Don't worry. I won't let you down. Just watch. The competition will be a cakewalk."

His words stimulated a smile in return. "I believe you and in you," I said.

"So you'll come and teach me every Sunday morning?"

I nodded. "Okay. That's fine."

We were close to number 4 now, so I bade him farewell. But he said, "Come, I want to show you something."

I hesitated, but there was no pickup in the driveway, so I followed.

We went in through the garage, and he told me to wait in the kitchen.

I looked around. The dishes were washed. The napkins were folded and neatly stacked on the counter, which gleamed in the sunlight. The floor was probably clean enough to lie on. As there was nothing to catch my interest, I began to hear soft music drifting in from the living room.

Thinking that was what Wolf had wanted to show me, I swung open the kitchen door. There I found, not Wolf, but Junior and an older woman who looked like she was his mother. He had an arm around her waist, while he held her hand with another. They made little squares as they danced around the room.

"That's all there is to it, Ma," he said to her.

She was smiling from ear to ear. "I like it. It's nice. I should follow you one day."

I tried to step back into the kitchen, but Wolf emerged from the corridor, banging the door behind him. That made them turn.

"Oh, hello," Junior said with a smile.

"Hi," I replied with a wave. And then I turned slightly to his mother. "Good afternoon."

"Good afternoon," she replied. "Please, you are?"

"My name is Desire Mensah," I said. "I just moved into number 3, and I teach at your son's school." I pointed to Wolf.

"Oh so you're our new neighbor!" she exclaimed. "I'm Adjoa, Adjoa Ofori. It's nice to meet you."

I smiled. "It's nice to meet you. Your son said he had something to show me, so I came over."

"Oh, that's okay. We're happy to have you over."

Wolf tugged at my arm. "Come, come, come," he said.

"I'm sorry," I told his mother. "Your son wants me to follow him."

She laughed. "That one, that's the way he is. He's so insistent when he wants something. You let him show you what he wants to."

"Thank you," I said. Then I allowed Wolf to pull me into the kitchen.

"Look at this," he said, and placed a large sheet of cardboard on the counter. "Look what I made."

It was a mosaic of a house on a hill. "Oh, this is nice, Wolf," I said.

He beamed with pride.

I took a closer look. "You made the image out of little colored paper triangles."

"Yes," he nodded. "I got the idea while reading about how 3D images are rendered on computers, and I thought it would be nice to try something like it with the mosaic."

The mosaic had a blue sky, an orange sun, and white clouds over the house. The house itself was made out of rust-red triangles, and beside the house stood two stick figures holding hands.

"Who are they?" I asked.

"I don't know. There was this old white lady who visited our class one day. And she had a similar mosaic with her that she showed to the class, and there were two people in it. So I made two people."

"Oh, okay. Who was the old lady?"

"Her name was Lavinia. She was an artist."

"That's a lovely name."

"She died a few months after visiting us."

"Oh, that's too bad."

"'So it goes,'" he said with a giggle.

I saw the joke and laughed along.

"What's so funny?" asked Junior, stepping into the kitchen.

"Nothing," Wolf said. He picked up his mosaic and held it to his chest. "It's between just me and Desire."

Junior chuckled as he reached into the fridge and picked a bottle of water. "Okay, young man. Nobody bore."

"Go back and dance like a little girl," grumbled Wolf.

Junior and I laughed and caught each other's eye. "You can waltz, I see," I said to him.

"I'm now learning," he replied.

"Okay."

"The classes are every weekend. They teach the waltz, the tango, salsa, and even the jive. We could go together if you want."

He was selling, but after what had happened with Addison, I was in no mood to buy.

"Thanks, but I'm not much of a dancer," I said.

"Oh, some of them are really easy to learn. I'm a beginner myself."

I shook my head. "That's nice, but I'm sorry."

"Okay. Well, I'm going to continue teaching my mother. I'll see you."

"See you."

5

―――

"WHY WOULD YOU DO SUCH A THING?" ASKED MY mother that Saturday when I told her about Junior's invitation. "You, you think you're growing younger, eh?"

Of course I couldn't tell her about Addison, so I just said, "I wasn't interested, Ma."

"Love can grow. Love grows with time. Even sometimes you have to fake it small."

I switched the receiver to my other ear and sighed. "Yes, Ma."

"You be there and 'Yes, Ma' me. Don't you know that people like that don't get married? You shouldn't be so choosy and picky. Haven't you seen Auntie Dorothy? You see the way she has become?"

"Ma, ah!"

"Be quiet. You, you don't think about the future. You don't care about me koraa. How can my mind rest when you're not married? You better find someone you're interested in. Or me I will look for one for you. I've said my own. Goodbye."

"Bye, Ma."

I limped back to my bedroom and threw myself into bed. The cramps were awful, as they always had been ever since I was nine.

My mother just didn't understand. She imagined I was waiting for some knight in shining armor to come sweep me off my feet. And while that would be nice, that wasn't it. Half of the men I met cared more about themselves than me. And the other half cared more about me than us.

I hadn't even made myself comfortable when the phone rang again. I hauled myself back out of bed and to the living room.

"Hello?"

"Sweetie, good morning."

"Who is this?"

"Ah, so you don't know my voice?"

"I'm sorry. Please who are you?"

"Herh, sweetie, I shock give you oh. So you don't know my voice. I'm offended."

"I said I'm sorry. Just tell me who this is. People sound different over the telephone, and I'm having a bad—"

"You have to make it up to me, sweetie."

"Please don't call me that."

"Make it up to me, sweetie, and I'll tell you who I am."

"Fine. How?"

"Call me darling."

I kissed my teeth. "No. I'm going to hang up now."

"No, wait! Okay I'll tell you. It's me, Gerald."

I almost banged the receiver. "What do you want, Gerald?"

"Ei, can't I call my sweetie and fine out how she's doing?"

"Gerald, I'm not your sweetie. Stop it. How did you even get my telephone number?"

"You too you're stubborn oh."

"How did you get my number, Gerald?"

I heard him laugh. "I have my ways. And wherever there is a will, or I should say a desire rather, there is a way."

I sighed. "Okay, Gerald. So what do you want?"

"I just called to check up on you and see how you're doing."

"Okay. I'm fine. I'll see you on—"

"Wait! Do you know what I'm calling you on? It's not a landline."

"A payphone?"

"A mobile phone."

I could imagine him grinning smugly and foolishly. "That's good for you."

"My auntie in Germany sent it down."

"Okay."

"I paid one million just to get the sim from Kasatel."

"Wow." I wasn't at all impressed.

"Yeah, but how you go do am, chale?"

"Yeah."

"So what are you doing this evening? Let me go and spread you, eh? I'll do you like butter."

"No, please, Gerald. I have no plans to leave my house."

"Oh, why?"

"I'm not well."

"Oh, then I will come and take care of you."

"No. Gerald, don't. I'm okay. I don't need help."

"Come on, tell me where you stay."

"I won't. Your time is important. Don't worry about me."

"No, sweetie. You are important to me. I want—"

The conversation had gone on long enough.

"There's someone at my door. I have to go. Bye."

I slammed the receiver.

After taking three tablets of paracetamol, I went back to bed.

It was late afternoon when I awoke. Feeling much better, I took a shower and settled in front of the television. To my amazement, I could catch only GTV. They weren't showing anything worth watching, so I poured myself a glass of wine and started to mark some test papers.

At about half past six, there was a banging at my door. I got the door without any idea that I would find Gerald standing there with a black polythene bag in his hand.

"Sweetie!" he exclaimed with a ridiculous grin he imagined was alluring.

"Gerald? How did you find my house?"

"Wherever there's a desire, there's a way," he said, taking my hand off the doorpost and walking in. "Ei, you still haven't unpacked. See all these suitcases."

I just stood there, hands on hips.

"So you had a party and didn't call me," he said, picking up an empty bottle of Cabernet Franc from a stack near the door.

He looked at me and I glared at him. He then relaxed himself in my seat and started going through my test papers.

"These children, demma head die pass," he said with a chuckle.

I balanced myself on the arm of my sofa with a sigh.

"Ei sweetie, so you won't offer me water sef?"

"What do you want, Gerald?" I asked.

"I came to see how you're doing." He reached down and took his mobile phone out of the pouch on his belt. "See my new phone? It's a Sony Ericsson."

"No, I won't, Gerald. What do you want?"

He regarded me for a while. From my eyes, his gaze dropped lower to my chest, then even lower, and then back to my eyes again. "You really aren't feeling well."

"What?"

"All this cold feedback I'm getting from you. You really must not be feeling well."

"Yes, I'm not. So I'd really appreciate it if—"

He sprung up from his seat. "That's why I brought this." He reached into his polythene bag and brought out a VHS tape. "It's Nana Banyin's new movie, *Mpanyinsɛm*. Abi you've heard of it?"

"No."

"Well, you'll love it," he said. "You have a deck, right? Off the light and let's watch it."

The VCR sat right beside my TV. I had to think quickly. "It's not working."

But he was quicker. He had already started to insert the cassette. After setting up the movie, he flopped back into my sofa and then tugged on my arm to join him.

Mustering all the patience humanly possible, I dropped down into the seat beside him. I figured I would try to make the best of the situation by at least trying to enjoy the movie.

After less than half an hour, I was completely fed up. And not just because the movie was poorly written, poorly directed, poorly acted, and poorly produced, but because Gerald kept on placing a hand on my knee or thigh or around my shoulder.

"I'll be back soon," I told him.

He was too engrossed in the movie to care.

I pulled on my favorite hoodie, which I had pinched from Mike's house, and walked out of the house into the cool night air.

I had no idea where I was going, but anywhere was better than inside with Gerald. When I got to the fork that branched off to number 4, Junior emerged. He was dressed up in a blue T-shirt folded up at the arms and black trousers held up by suspenders.

He looked in my direction, so I mouthed a "Hi" and waved before it occurred to me that he would be unable to see me.

He did manage to notice someone was there. He walked towards a now stationary me. When he got close, I lowered my hood and he said, "Oh it's you. Hi. How are you doing?"

"I'm okay. You're looking good. Are you going somewhere?"

He grinned and looked down at himself. "Thanks. Dancing class. The one I told you about."

"Oh yeah. You said it was on weekends. I forgot."

"No worries." His hands were in his pockets now. He looked about. "So what are you doing out?"

"Oh, uhm . . . " I paused to think up a lie, and just as I opened my mouth to spill it out, he started to say something, interrupting me.

He was quick to apologize. "I'm sorry. Please go on."

For some reason, the truth rolled easily off my tongue. "I'm hiding from someone."

He chuckled. "I see. You should pay your debts, you know."

I could not stop myself from laughing out loud. "No. It's not like that. He's after something else."

"I see. Give me a moment," he said.

He went round the back of his house and emerged with a bench, which he set down in front of the garage door. He gestured that I join him.

"Aren't you going to be late?" I asked as I sat down beside him.

"Oh, don't worry. These are Ghanaians we're talking about. You know how Ghana man time is like."

I giggled. "Oh yes. Six o'clock is seven thirty."

That made him smile. "Besides, ten minutes won't make much difference."

"Okay."

"I'm sure after ten minutes, it would be safe for you to return home."

My giggle turned to laughter. "This guy? I don't think so. He's persistent."

"Or would you like me to go get rid of him? I have macho," he said, flexing his muscles.

"Hoh!"

He smiled. "Touch it and see."

I poked his arm. "Yeah, you do. And that would be so, so nice. Unfortunately, he's a coworker, so I can't afford to antagonize him too strongly. Let's just wait for him to leave."

We could see my porch from our vantage point, so we sat there waiting for Gerald to surrender my home. In the meantime, Junior told me about himself. He was an artist. I thought that was really cool.

"Yeah, but not everyone approves," he said with a grimace.

"I think I understand."

"The old man really wants me to practice instead."

"Practice what?"

"I'm a medical doctor by profession."

"Wow." It was genuine this time.

"So tell me, Miss Desire, why you came out here."

I was starting to tell him about my getting a job at the JSS when the lights suddenly went out.

"Oh ECG!" came a cry from inside the house.

My mind immediately went to Gerald alone in my house, and I rose.

"You want to leave?"

"Yes, I've got to make sure—" I stopped. I didn't really care. "No. I don't actually. I'm enjoying myself here."

The moon was a thin crescent, so the darkness was almost complete. But my eyes had adjusted to the dark a bit, and I could see the outline of a smile on his face. "Let me go and get us a candle," he said.

"Okay." Then I called after him, "Do you have any wine, Junior?"

"Wine?"

"Yes. I was having a glass when that guy came and interrupted me."

He laughed. "Don't worry, we've got a bottle of red wine stowed away somewhere."

"My favorite kind."

Soon he was back. He sat down facing me with a leg on either side. He lighted the candle and stuck it to a saucer, which he set down between us. I turned to face him while he placed a glass in front of me.

"What about you?" I asked as he filled the glass.

He shook his head. "I don't drink alcohol."

I took a gulp. "I rarely drink myself."

"So you were telling me why you came here?"

"Oh yes, erm, there was nothing for me back in Accra," I said.

"Rather? When that's where everyone wants to go because there's nothing here."

My lips curled in imitation of a smile. "I lost a lot of things in Accra. My father died and we lost our property and I lost my job."

"Oh, sorry. I didn't know."

"Don't worry," I said with a shrug. I took another gulp and set the empty glass down. "So here I am." I picked up the bottle and refilled the glass. "Besides, I don't like city life."

"Why? I miss Accra so much. We used to live there as well."

"Really?"

"Yeah. We lived in Tema until '88. My father then took a job as a lecturer at the university, so we had to move here." He paused for a moment. "Shortly after we moved, my mother found out she was pregnant. It was an accident. It wasn't planned. Well, she delivered and Kwabena was born and—"

"Sorry, Kwabena?"

"Wolfgang."

"Oh, Wolf. I see."

"He has managed to get you to call him Wolf, eh? That's his new thing now. That boy, eh."

"I like him," I said. "Anyway, go on with your story."

He did. "After she had given birth to him, the hospital gave her painkillers to help her sleep. They were expired."

My mouth dropped open.

"She died."

"No!" I exclaimed. "And what happened to the doctors and nurses? I hope they went to jail or were sacked." My emotions had me leaning forward.

He shook his head calmly. "We gave it to God."

I sat back and pressed my lips together. The words which threatened to come out of my mouth would not be thought of as wholesome or becoming of a lady.

"You can let your words fly," he said with a laugh. "We've insulted them saah. Yours would just be a drop in the ocean."

Even though his words moved me to laughter, my eyes watered.

"Are you crying?" he asked in disbelief.

I wiped my eyes and took a large gulp of wine. "I'm sorry. I had a . . . a brother who died, that's why."

"Sorry."

"He was just a baby. Don't mind me, okay." I took another gulp. "Let's change the topic."

"Okay," he said. "Look up."

I did and gasped. A brilliant silver shroud was spread across the sky. There seemed to be thousands upon thousands of stars out. I had never seen anything like it before.

"It's beautiful," I whispered.

"You don't see this in Accra," he said.

"You certainly don't."

He put out the candle. "We won't need this now."

"Look, some have colors! That one is reddish."

He chuckled. "Yeah."

I tapped his thigh. "Look, look. Look at those three stars in a line there."

"That's Orion's belt," he replied. "And that red one you saw, that's his shoulder."

I looked back down at him.

"In Greek mythology, Orion is a mighty hunter." He took my hand and traced the outline of Orion's body. "And that one there, the one that looks blueish is his leg."

"Wow."

"According to the story, Orion fell in love with Merope, the daughter of Oenopion the king of Chios, and wanted to marry her. But Oenopion was opposed to the marriage. Orion attempted to seize Merope by force, but the giant scorpion, Scorpio, stung Orion and killed him."

He turned me around and pointed to an even redder star. "And those stars right there, they are Scorpio. They are on opposite sides of the sky to avoid further conflict between the two."

I was impressed. "How does a medical doctor know this?"

"My mother had a keen interest in the stars and also in the stories around them. She had many books on them. Kwabena has chewed them all and will never let anyone rest."

"Oh, okay. That certainly sounds like him."

"He's a good kid. Want to hear some more?"

I nodded.

"Did you just nod in the dark?" he asked, trying to hold back laughter.

I laughed as well. "Mmai! But you saw me, didn't you?"

He took my hand again and pointed at what looked like a small, elongated cloud. "It would be much easier to see with a pair of binoculars, but that's Andromeda."

"That's a galaxy, right? And what's the story behind it?"

"Andromeda was the daughter of Cepheus and Cassiopeia, who ruled over Ethiopia. Cassiopeia claimed to be more beautiful than Juno, the wife of Jupiter. In response to the insult, Neptune sent a sea monster to destroy the city. The only way to stop the destruction was for Cepheus to sacrifice the beautiful Andromeda to the monster. So she was chained to a slab of rock for the monster to devour."

"Oh!"

"Fortunately, Perseus swoops down from the sky and saves Andromeda. They get married and presumably live happily ever after."

"How delightful," I said after swallowing a mouthful of wine. "I'm sure she bore him ten sons and ten daughters. I'm sure—" I stopped abruptly. The cramps were suddenly back.

Junior noticed. "Is there a problem?"

"I'm not feeling too good."

He got up and came over to my side. "Let me take you home. I think your friend should be gone by now."

I grabbed hold of his arm and we made our way slowly over to my bungalow. Gerald was thankfully nowhere to be found.

As Junior bade me goodnight, he handed me the bottle of wine. "It's a gift," he said. "It's also nearly empty."

I laughed. "Thank you."

He started to walk back towards his house when I called out to him, "You missed your class tonight. I just remembered. I'm so sorry."

"Don't worry," he called back. "This was just as fun. I hope I managed to make your evening bearable."

I smiled to myself.

"I hope you're nodding in the dark again, Desire Mensah," he said from somewhere out in the night.

I was.

6

HAVING TAKEN IN NOTHING BUT WINE THE NIGHT
before, I awoke the next morning with a rumbling tummy. I
checked the box of instant noodles I had brought along with
me and found nothing but empty sachets. So I walked downhill
to the main road and hailed a taxi. I hoped I would get some
waakye to buy despite it being a Sunday. After less than a minute,
I saw a filling station with a mart attached to it. I alighted there.

I picked up a few loaves of bread, a box of apple-flavored tea,
milk, sugar, ketchup, corned beef, tuna flakes, two more boxes of
instant noodles, several cans of potato chips, and a couple bottles
of Carménère. The cashier, a nice young man who said his name
was Gabriel, helped me load my stuff into a taxi.

When I got home, the driver was also nice enough to help
me carry everything to my kitchen. He gave me his mobile
number in case I needed a ride anywhere.

After eating a bowl of noodles, I picked up a few textbooks
and went over to Wolf's. I found him home alone.

"They've gone to church," he said.

We carried a blackboard from the garage and set it up on the porch.

"You didn't want to go with them?" I asked as I wiped the board.

"Daddy said I should stay behind and study. His god makes exceptions, I guess."

"Okay."

"Besides, 'Religion is the opiate of the masses.' Karl Marx."

I laughed so hard I doubled over. It did not surprise me one bit. "You don't believe in religion, then?"

"Not really. However, I think I might decide to be religious soon."

I chuckled. "Why?"

"Atheism is in fashion now. All the sheep are jumping on the disbelief express."

"Well, we have a lot more scientific knowledge to explain the world. It's enough for some people."

He made a sound indicating disgust and frowned. "If the conformists decide to build a bridge across the river, I'll build my bridge along it. But what really interests me is—"

I turned. "Is?"

"Why God would make humans so pathetic."

"We are?"

"Not on a biological level, of course. Humans are marvels of engineering. But up here." He pointed to his head. "There's something wrong with them. They don't make sense."

"Well, this isn't what God made," I said.

"He made a mistake when he made me a man."

"I'm sure wolves would be quite happy with the ability to question their makeup."

His eyebrows furrowed. "No, not that way. I wish I wasn't male."

"Ah, why?"

He linked his fingers together and rested his chin upon them. "Female just seems much better. The male gender is so ..." He touched his lip and thought for a while. "... so weak. I don't quite know how to articulate it yet. The idea hasn't incubated in my head for too long."

I chuckled. "I'd like to see your father's face when he hears that."

Wolf laughed along. "They just say I'm insane."

"Doesn't that hurt you?"

He looked up at me, bemused. "No, they just don't understand, really. If anything, I feel pity for them. Because, you know, they are dumb."

I just stared at him and smiled, while a warm feeling saturated my chest. Junior was right, he was a good kid.

"You know his ex was also an English teacher?" he asked.

"Who?"

"Junior."

"Really? What happened? They broke up?"

"No, she drank chloroxylenol."

"Huh?"

"Disinfectant," he said with a little grin.

"What!?"

"Yeah. She was a weak little thing. It wasn't surprising to me, of course."

"Why did she do it?"

He shrugged. "She bit off more than she could chew, I guess."

"When did this happen?"

"Oh, about a year and a half ago. He never speaks of her."

"Of course he wouldn't," I said. "It must have been terrible for him."

"She finished the entire bottle, you know? She was determined," he said, laughing. "That was about the only thing she did in her life with any sort of resolve."

I frowned. And upon his noticing it, his laughter died away. "I think we should get to work now," I said. "We only have now until Tuesday to get ready."

"Sure."

I taught Wolf nothing new that morning. His grasp of the English language was probably just as good as mine. It wasn't a waste of my time, because when the Oforis returned from church, I got to notice for the first time just how handsome Junior was.

"His structure is similar to Akwasi's," I told my mother later. "Tall and very well built but not with so much muscle. His is nice. Is he dark or fair? Not too dark. And not fair either. He's chocolate, sort of. He likes wearing suspenders, and they are so cool. But Ma, you should see his eyes. They are really light brown. When he shook my hand and I looked into his eyes, I almost melted."

"Ah. So if he's this handsome, why did you turn him down the last time?"

"I wasn't in the mood. Ma, besides, it's not about looks. My soul has to connect with him."

"Nonsense. Any two people can make a marriage work. Do you know that the landlord is increasing the rent? Ten percent."

"Oh! How can he?"

"You don't know. Do you know what Akosua told me last time? She said Jeff has bought a new house at East Legon. He was handsome, a good Christian, and rich. If you had accepted his proposal, we wouldn't have these problems."

"Hmm . . . "

"You be there and be turning men down. If he asks you to go out with him again, you better be in the mood. You think it's only you who has seen that he's handsome?"

I sighed. "Yes, Ma."

7

THE FIRST ROUND OF THAT YEAR'S *WONDERKIDS* WAS hosted in the assembly hall. Even though that Tuesday had been declared a half day, the entire school, from primary to senior secondary, tried to cram itself into a hall built to hold just a hundred people.

Those who had arrived an hour early managed to get seats. Those who arrived three quarters of an hour early managed to squeeze themselves onto the edges of the benches. Those who arrived half an hour early sat on the floor in front of the first row of seats. Those who arrived a quarter of an hour early found themselves having to huddle around windows. I arrived with five minutes to spare. Baiden gave up his seat for me. But this was after Gerald offered me a place on his lap.

All the excitement and suspense that had been building up erupted into cheers and applause when Wolf walked into the room. I laughed as he bowed and waved to the crowd. Jama chants might have broken out at that point if the teachers hadn't silenced the crowd. The arrival of his teammates, two form three students from the secondary school, barely even registered with the crowd.

The winner of the contest was obvious by the end of the first round. Wolf had answered six out of the ten questions asked. The contest ended with a resounding 18,500 to 2,000 victory for Lighthouse Academy, with Wolf responsible for 17,500 of those points.

"You were fantastic, Wolf. You could actually win the competition!" I said to him once Madam Fire-Eater had released him from her office.

"I appreciate you covering me in your epithelial cells," he grumbled. "Thank God horizontal DNA transfer is not a thing in large multicellular organisms."

"Come on! This is a special occasion. You more than held your own against kids much older than you."

He made a face. "It's not special. I didn't get a perfect score. Winning is nothing without the perfect score."

"Winning alone is a big enough deal," I said.

"So many others have won in the past."

"But these guys are way above your level."

He stopped walking and looked at me like I had spoken a great and almost unforgiveable insult.

"Wow, I'm sorry. How about I buy you something nice?"

His face lit up. "Like?"

"What do you want?"

A yogurt seller rode past the school gate on his bicycle, sounding his horn.

"Erm, yogurt would be nice," he said.

I chuckled. "Yes, sir!"

We ate the yogurt as we walked home.

"Will you be coming over to see Junior?" he asked me.

"Why would you ask me that?"

"I saw and heard the two of you last time."

"On Saturday?"

"Yes."

"Okay."

"It was obvious you were both enjoying each other's company."

I shrugged. "Your brother is a nice guy."

"It won't work out, you know. The two of you are too different."

This made me laugh hard. I clapped my hands together. "I had no idea you were a matchmaker as well. You're a man of many talents, I see."

A little smile appeared on the corner of his mouth. "It was just the darkness. The warm feelings you have won't withstand the glare of daylight."

"I never said I had warm feelings for him."

"It's obvious."

My heart skipped a beat.

"Not to him, of course," he continued. "He's a typical guy; he doesn't see anything beyond his nose. It's clear to me, though."

I tried hard not to let my relief show.

When we reached our junction, I followed him along the path to his house. There was no pickup in the driveway. "And how is it clear to you?" I asked. "You're just a child."

He didn't reply immediately. Instead he opened the garage door and entered, leaving me outside. A moment later, the door opened just wide enough for me to see his face. Then he said, "I watch you, Desire. I watch you all the time." Then he shut the gate.

I stood there for a while.

When I was thirteen, I spent a month with my aunt who lived in Teshie because my mother wanted me to be "domesticated." There was a man next door, an old man who they said went to Burma to fight. He had a bad leg, so he would lean against his wall and watch my cousin and I play ampe. He never spoke, but his gaze was unsettling. On my last night there, I woke up to find a shadow by my bedroom window. I watched in petrified silence as it tried unsuccessfully to open the window and then limped away.

The memory sent a shiver down my spine.

I was just about to leave when Junior stepped out of the boys' quarters.

"Hello, Desire," he said with a wide smile.

"Hello, Junior," I replied. "Are you working?" The denim overalls he wore were covered in paint of all colors.

He looked down at himself and back at me. "Yes. The boys' quarters double as my studio. I came out to take a break and get some fresh air."

"Okay," I said, wondering if my attraction to him was indeed obvious.

"Would you like to see some of my work?" he asked.

"Sure!" After all, who cared if he could tell that I liked him?

"I'm messing around with oil paint, so please excuse the clutter," he said as he stepped inside. "I normally work with pastel, but I want to try something new."

The corridor the front door opened into was littered with cans of paint and what smelt to me like turpentine. Clumsy me stumbled over one, but Junior grabbed my arm quickly.

"Thanks."

Still holding onto me—he was holding my hand, actually—he led me into the room where he created his art. I had little exposure to art, but it was obvious he was quite good. There were beautiful landscapes of all sorts.

One painting caught my eye. It was of a lighthouse on the edge of a cliff with a raging sea below.

He noticed my interest and said, "That's Cape Three Points."

"Oh really? I didn't know. I've never been there."

"You must visit it sometime," he said. "It's a wonderful place. It's one of my favorite places in Ghana."

"You've been to many places in the country?" I asked him.

He nodded, picked up another painting, and handed it to me. "This is Lake Bosumtwe."

This one was even more amazing than the lighthouse. The sparkling blue lake lay at the bottom of the crater, with the walls, green with vegetation, towering high above.

"This is actually my favorite place in Ghana," Junior said.

"You are really good. When did you start painting?"

He shifted his weight backwards and scratched the back of his head to think. My, was he handsome in that pose.

"Well, I've been drawing as long as I can remember, but I started to paint probably around ten." He retrieved a stool and offered it to me.

I sat down. "I think it's good you developed your talent. Most people don't."

He shrugged. "I probably may have been way better if I hadn't thrown away seven years of my life in med school. I hope you don't mind if I work while we chat."

"Oh no, not at all. So why did you go to med school, then?"

He leaned forward and started to draw. "Well, pressure from teachers and friends and family, I guess. Being a doctor comes with a certain level of respect, you know. And my father threatened to disown me if I didn't." He chuckled.

"Really? He would go that far?"

"The old man does not like to be defied." He pulled back his left sleeve to reveal a dark triangular scar on his forearm. "I got this because I skipped school once."

"What did that?"

"A hot knife," he replied. "For not wanting to go to med school I got fifteen lashes on my back to help me change my mind."

I don't know how he managed to say that with a smile on his face. "That's . . . "

"Horrible, right? You can say it. I don't mind."

"Yes, it is!"

My thoughts shifted to Wolf. "What about your brother?"

"What about him?"

"Did your father force him to be on *Wonderkids?*"

Junior laughed. "Of course not. Kwabena loves stuff like that. He's a driven child. He likes to learn, and he's competitive as well. The old man is proud of him."

I shifted uncomfortably in my seat.

"Desire," said Junior. "Say what's on your mind. Don't worry."

"He's a child!" I blurted out. "Let him be a child. This is too much for him. It will be. I know it."

"No one is forcing him. He wants to do it. This is what he's good at. Why shouldn't he fulfill his potential? I wish I had."

I sagged my shoulders and sighed. "Okay. I guess you're right. I don't know, I'm just protective of him."

"It's your motherly instincts," he said with a smile.

I returned the smile, unconvincingly.

Junior noticed. "Is there something wrong?"

I shook my head and put on a more convincing smile. "Oh no, there's nothing wrong." I even added a little laugh.

He stared at me with a skeptical expression. "I feel I went somewhere I shouldn't have. Or you don't want to have children? Is that it?"

That made me laugh out loud. "Of course I do. Why would you think such a thing?"

He smiled and shrugged. "Some women don't."

"That's them; me, I do papa. I want five little boys."

"Herh!" he exclaimed.

"Why?"

"You don't want to sleep, eh? Boys are troublesome oh. You didn't even say one, but five."

I laughed. "I guess it's because I was an only child."

"So you'll want to get married then?"

"Ah. Why not? How do you see me, Junior?"

He raised his arms in mock surrender. "Oh no, it's just I heard my old man worrying you the other time about not wanting to get married. And it seems to me that you don't have a boyfriend. You weren't even half interested in that other guy who came to see you."

I laughed so hard that I snorted, and that only made me laugh harder. It took me a full minute to get myself under control. "Gerald? I'll never be interested in Gerald for anything."

"Oh, why?" Junior asked. "He begs." I noticed a smile hiding somewhere in his expression.

"He could grovel for all I care."

"Okay, at least give him some small attention, eh?"

I shook my head. Feeling a little honest, I said, "I only give my time to people I like . . . to be around."

His eyes left the canvas and met mine for a fleeting moment. But a moment was all that was needed for our eyes to say the words our lips didn't. His attention returned to the canvas, but a dimple appeared in his cheeks as he smiled to himself.

There was silence now. The only sound was the pencil scratching against the canvas and my heart beating in my ears.

Then he spoke. "How would you like to have dinner with us this evening, Desire?"

8

"HELLO, MA."

"Desire. How are you?"

"I'm fine, Ma. I have news for you," I said. "Ma, he invited me to dinner with his family this evening."

"Really? That's good," she said, but her voice was flat and unenthusiastic. "I also have some news for you."

"What is it?"

Now life entered her voice. "Jeff came by the house today."

I shook my head. "And what does he want?"

"Oh, he was asking how we're coping with life, the rent and everything."

"Okay."

"He asked about you too."

That was no surprise. "And what did you tell him, Ma?"

"I told him you were okay. And that you are still single."

"Oh, Ma. Why did you do that?"

"See, he came to the house with the latest Benz. I'm talking about a 1999 license plate oh."

"So what? Ma, I don't like him. He's so arrogant."

"Why shouldn't he be arrogant when he can afford to change cars every six months? I told you about the rent advance, didn't I?"

"I'll send you some money as soon as we're paid."

"It won't be enough. You know that."

"Beg the landlord. Tell him we'll pay the rest later."

"This one koraa, he has tried for us. You know it's only because he knew your father that's why he gave the place to us at half the price, right?"

"Hmm . . ."

"Anyway, Jeff said he's traveling to the UK but when he returns he'll pass by and visit you."

I kissed my teeth. "I hope he doesn't. Anyway, I've got to go, Ma. I'll call you later."

After taking a bath, I changed into something more comfortable, leggings and a plaid blouse, and I held my braids in a ponytail. I didn't want them flying around and being a nuisance.

Junior said they would be eating fufu and light soup that evening. He asked me if I would like to pound, but I laughed hard and told him no. Fufu was only nice when you didn't have to pound. Also, I asked him not to add the normal amount of pepper to the soup. A few nasty experiences had left me wary.

I smelt the light soup when I got to their driveway. It promised to taste good. Junior got the door and led me in through the kitchen, where Mrs. Ofori was hard at work. She smiled at me and I dropped a little curtsy.

In the dining room, Junior gave me a seat opposite Wolf, who had his hands under his cheeks and was pouting.

"What's wrong?" I asked.

He did not even look up at me, but when his mother entered the room carrying a bowl of soup he moaned, "Mummy, I'm hungry."

His mother set the bowl down on the dining table. "Kwabena, you know we can't start without your father."

"He's late today," added Junior, setting down another.

"I wonder what's keeping him," Mrs. Ofori said on her way back to the kitchen.

Junior then bent over and whispered in my ear, "Won't you like to help out in the kitchen?"

I laughed. "Oh no, if you'd like to enjoy the meal, you won't want me anywhere near it," I joked. "Besides, you guys look like you have everything under control."

He smiled. "Okay. No problem."

The landline rang. "Kwabena, answer the phone!" called Mrs. Ofori from the kitchen.

Mumbling all the way, Wolf went and answered it. "Hello, Ofori residence." His demeanor then changed. He straightened up and his voice came out cheerful. "Oh, hello, Daddy. Okay. Okay. Bye, Daddy."

Wolf walked over to the kitchen. "Mummy, Daddy said he's leaving the office. He'll be home in a few minutes."

"Okay."

After laying the table, Junior took his seat beside Wolf. Mrs. Ofori took hers at one end, leaving the other for Mr. Ofori. Wolf buried his nose in an organic chemistry textbook while Mrs. Ofori started to mend a shirt and hum to herself.

"Nice fingernails," Junior said.

"Thanks," I said. "I was bored and felt like doing something different, so I decided to paint them matte black. Normally they would be dark red or navy blue."

He took my fingers in his hands and examined them. "It works quite nicely with your skin color. This is the first time I've seen you with painted nails."

I shrugged. "I wasn't in the mood until recently."

His attention now shifted to my face. "I never noticed that before."

"What?"

"That scar just under your ear."

"Oh, that." I touched the scar instinctively. It was a sort of thin crescent under my right ear. "It's a relic of my Motown days."

"You went to Achimota?"

"Yes. My friend and I snuck out of our house one night to meet my crush, Elorm. He was in Lugard house, so I had to go all the way to the East to meet him. We were around the hospital when we saw the senior house mistress coming in her car. We decided to run, and of course, me being so clumsy, I fell over into some bushes. A twig then gave it to me."

He laughed.

"You're laughing? When we got back to the house my friend applied alcohol to it and it stung, papa. I cried myself to sleep."

"So what's the moral of the story?" he asked.

"I should look where I'm going next time?"

He chuckled. "Next time let the boys come to you rather."

"Oh, get away." I pretended to throw something at him.

All of a sudden, Wolf jumped up. "Daddy's in!" he proclaimed and made for the garage.

I then heard it, the sound of tires over gravel and the deep and steady roar of the large pickup engine. I heard the garage door being unlocked and then swinging on rusty hinges. Then the engine was turned off. The pickup truck door slammed. The kitchen door squeaked open and then shut. Wolf appeared with his father's briefcase, which he set down, and returned to the table. Mr. Ofori entered the room a moment later. He had that habit really tall people had of stooping slightly as he entered the room although he could have walked upright through the door. He landed heavily in his chair at the head of the table.

"You're welcome, Da," said Mrs. Ofori.

Mr. Ofori grunted a reply as he dragged his seat forward.

Then, as if on cue, everyone bowed their heads.

After Mr. Ofori said a prayer, I said to Junior, "Could I please have a spoon? I don't like to eat with my hands."

Activity around the table stopped for a moment. Only Wolf started to eat.

"Sure," Junior said eventually. "I'll go get it."

"Thanks."

Mr. Ofori's eyes followed Junior out of the room, and he muttered something under his breath. He stuck his fingers into the fufu and, after tearing a handful away from the main lump, he scooped up the soup in a way I never could understand, let alone master.

The moment the food met his tongue, he dropped his hand to the table with a thud. "Adjoa, what is this?"

"Our guest doesn't like pepper," Mrs. Ofori replied.

His eyes were wide and fierce. I feared he might jump out of his seat at any moment. "So you couldn't prepare mine separately?"

"I'm sorry," I said, but I was ignored.

"Is the guest more important than the man of the house?" He brought down his other fist hard.

Mrs. Ofori shot him a pleading look.

Wolf then spoke up. "I won today, Daddy."

Immediately, he turned to his son. "Ah yes, and what was your score?"

"Eighteen thousand, five hundred points. Some of the questions were difficult because—"

"You were 11,500 points short. You must study more. You must get that scholarship. Have you heard? You have no excuse whatsoever. I never had the advantages you have. My father refused to send me to school because he wanted help on his farm.

I had to run away when I was sixteen. Yet I was able to get a full scholarship at Oxford. You've been too playful and distracted of late. You better sit up."

"Yes, Daddy."

"And this one?" He pointed his jaw in the direction of Junior, who was returning with the spoon. Before Junior could say anything, he continued. "What else would he do but sit in that dirty room and draw? A thirty-year-old man." He shook his head. "It's a disgrace."

"I also wrote an essay today, Daddy," interjected Wolf again.

Junior took his seat and handed the spoon over to me.

"About what?" Mr. Ofori enquired gruffly.

"I wrote about how male genital mutilation is an outmoded cultural practice and must be outlawed," replied Wolf with a proud smile on his face.

I set down the spoonful of fufu and light soup I was about to swallow. "Male genital mutilation?" I dared to ask, feeling it was my responsibility to lighten the mood.

"What you'll call circumcision," Wolf said.

His father's face darkened. "Have I not warned you about writing these kind of things? And what did you score?"

I could see Wolf deflate. "The teacher gave me eighty."

"What if she had given you a lower mark? At the end of the term, someone might take the prize for social studies. You better stop fooling with your future. You are too playful. You think you are still a child. I don't want to hear any such nonsense again."

His eyes surveyed the room in search of his next victim.

I picked up the spoonful of fufu I still had not eaten, trying to make myself inconspicuous.

"You," he barked at me.

The vehemence in his voice made me almost drop my spoon. I set it down again and turned to him.

"Would you marry a man like this one?" He pointed at Junior. "This layabout who does nothing but eat my food and leech on my money, claiming he is an artist."

"Well, erm, I don't think there's anything wrong—"

He kissed his teeth, loudly. "I don't even know why I asked you. You're birds of the same feather. This generation is doomed, Adjoa, doomed. I saw one lady on campus today wearing one of those things." He started to gesture around his stomach area.

"Show your stomach?" she suggested.

"Yes, that. Exposing herself just like the prostitutes at Kotokuraba."

Wolf spoke up again. "I read about redox reactions today, Daddy. I'm going to try and electroplate our cutlery with gold from Mummy's jewelry."

This time he was ignored. "All they know these days are fake nails, weaves or braids or whatever they call it, and leggings and short, short dresses and the rest. Empty-headed girls."

I looked down at my bowl.

"Who at all will marry these ones?" he continued. "Tell me, Miss Mensah, how old are you?," Mr. Ofori asked suddenly. I had to put down my spoon again, and my tummy rumbled in protest.

"Erm, I'm twenty-nine."

He turned to his wife and shook his head. "You see? Twenty-nine and unmarried? She should have been married by now. Ask her why."

"Don't attack her," Junior said in a low voice.

"Why shouldn't I? She's a perfect example of what I was talking about earlier, the degradation of our society. You be there and be following her painted nails and her hair and her makeup and see where she'll lead you to. Soon you'll be eating fufu with a spoon like a—"

Mrs. Ofori interrupted him with a loud cough.

He eyed his wife and then stood up abruptly, knocking the table and causing everything on its surface to jump. I had to hold my glass to stop it from falling over.

"Clear my plate, Adjoa," he commanded while washing his hand in the bowl of water before him. "I can't eat anymore of this this soup or whatever it is. I'm going to work, and I don't want to be disturbed."

He dried his hands with a napkin, threw it onto the table, and left the room.

The silence he left in his wake was loud and uncomfortable, too uncomfortable for me to handle certainly.

"I think I have to leave," I said.

"Oh no," Junior said, rising from his seat. "Don't mind my father."

"Oh, I'm fine."

I turned to Mrs. Ofori. "That was a lovely meal, and I enjoyed it." Turning back to Junior, I said, "I'll see you around."

He stood there and watched me find my way out.

I was so preoccupied with my thoughts that I did not notice I was not walking alone until I felt a hand slip into mine. It was Wolf. There was concern in his eyes. "My father can be a touch abrasive sometimes," he said.

Something salty touched my lip, and then I realized that a tear had gone down my face. I wiped it with the back of my hand.

"Here." He offered me a handkerchief.

We walked hand in hand and in silence until we got to the little gate. Wolf stood outside while I continued onto my porch.

As I fumbled with my keys he said to me, "They kill the person to save the woman."

"Okay, Wolf."

"That's what the humans do."

"Goodnight, Wolf."

Inside, I kicked off my shoes and fetched what turned out to be my penultimate bottle. I then settled on my couch to wallow in what little comfort I had in the quiet of the night.

9

I WAS ALREADY TWO HOURS LATE FOR WORK THE next morning when the rain started. After looking ominous for a while, the sky decided to let loose a downpour halfway into my walk. Initially, I was glad the rain had given me an excuse, but my umbrella could only do so much to protect me. The wind was so intense that each drop hurt like a sting.

When I arrived, cold and drenched, I was immediately informed by Baiden that Madam Fire-Eater had come looking for me.

"I see." Those were the first words out of Providencia Anaglate's mouth after I gingerly lowered myself into the seat before her desk.

My head throbbed. I muffled a burp.

The Fire-Eater frowned even harder. "Well, I've gone through Mr. Addison's papers, Miss Mensah, and I've found no documentation of your interview."

I swallowed hard.

"I also spoke with Mr. Gyamfi, and he says Addison asked him to hire you. That he had interviewed you himself and found you suitable for the position."

I couldn't help myself from rubbing my forehead.

"This is not how things are done, Miss Mensah."

"But I didn't do anything."

Providencia Anaglate sat back in her seat and watched me. Her glare made my headache ten times worse. After a while, she rose from her seat and leaned forward on her desk. "There's a certain kind of woman in this world, Miss Mensah. She's quite common, actually. This woman is nearly always very pretty, with good manners and always friendly, too friendly. This woman tends to move upwards surprisingly easily. I do not like this kind of woman."

A faint feeling of déjà vu came over me. I said nothing.

"You can leave now."

When I reached the door, she added, "I know who you are, Miss Mensah."

"Desire, what's wrong?" Felicia asked me when she found me bent over the bathroom sink, throwing up all the water I had drunk that morning.

I assured her I was fine and that it was just a little stomach upset. Laying my head down on my desk, I felt my life swinging inexorably towards catastrophe. My life felt like a pendulum, ever alternating between error and calamity. I got my water bottle and took a long drink.

As soon as the day was over, I made my way home, hastening past number 4. The silence of West End Ridge, which had once soothed me, was now overwhelming. I moved from my sofa to the window, taking a peek at my neighbors' house, and back to the sofa. Of course, nothing changed in the five-minute intervals between peeks.

I got out my address book and dialed Mike's number. We had been good friends in Legon. He walked me to my room after lectures every day. He was there when Nii broke up with me. He was by my side when I had my appendix taken out. He bought me chocolates every twenty-eight days. He said with my lifestyle, the cramps notifying me that I wasn't pregnant were a cause for celebration. And when I fought with my parents and wouldn't talk to them or go home, he took care of me the entire semester.

Ever since he got married we had drifted apart a bit, but I knew he'd be happy to hear from me. I called twice before realizing he would probably be at work. But it was no problem; he would call me back as soon as he could.

I then had a drink, cooked noodles, repainted my nails, and reread some old novels. When it was midnight and I could fight sleep no longer, I had a drink and dragged myself to bed.

The next day was just as dark and dreary as the day before, with the rain coming down steadily all day. Everyone was glad to have cool weather. I had always hated rain. Most people teased my so-called aborɔfosɛm. They said only crazy white people liked sunshine, but I preferred a dry warmth to cold, warmth like the feeling you get from a large teddy bear. Or a hug from your father. Or being wrapped up in the arms of your true love.

That day was payday, so after work I visited the filling station, craving something sweet. I got myself some strawberry wine. Wine was able to replicate that warm feeling to an extent. It was like that friend whose jollity was uplifting but, after a while, irritating, but who you'd still call again. So that night I had somewhat pleasing company while I waited for Mike. At midnight I went to bed.

It rained again for the third day in a row, although this time it reduced to a drizzle and eventually stopped by noon.

It was almost sunset when Mike finally called me back.

"Michael!"

"Hey, Desire, I've missed you."

"I've missed you much more, Mike. So, so, much. How have you been?"

"Swamped with work. Listen, I can't speak right now. Hannah and I going to that new restaurant in Labadi for our anniversary. How about I call you when I get home, okay?"

"Okay, sure. Say hi to—"

"We never say goodbye, Desire."

I smiled. "Till we meet again, Michael."

Then he hung-up.

I made my way to the kitchen and poured myself a glass of wine. I had just filled up the glass when I heard a knock at my door. All the things I wanted to say to Junior came flooding onto the tip of my tongue.

"Hello," said Wolf.

"Oh, it's you."

His smile faded a little. "Are you not happy to see me?"

"Of course I am." I took his hand. "Come on in."

"I thought you might be angry with me," he said, sitting down on my sofa.

I joined him. "Ah, why would I be?"

"Well, because of my father. You haven't looked for me since then."

"I've just been busy, that's why. Don't worry."

"Busy with what?" he asked, looking around.

I leaned back in the chair and looked at him, and I felt a tug in my heart. "You know what, Wolf, I was shy, that's why."

"Shy?" he asked.

"Your father said some hurtful things to me. And to some extent he was right."

He looked down at his feet and said nothing.

My eyes followed his, and I noticed that his trousers were short. He seemed too young for a growth spurt, but it wasn't impossible. In any case, he would need new trousers. I could get him a pair. And maybe a nice shirt to go with it.

"Have you eaten?" I asked him.

He shook his head. "I don't think I'll eat tonight."

"Oh, then let me get you something," I said, rising. Do you like potato chips?"

His face lit up. "Yes, yes. I love them. Uncle Max brings them from Accra whenever he visits. But Daddy never buys them. He says those are the things that make Americans fat and lazy."

He followed me to my fridge. I got the can and gave it to him. He opened it eagerly and began stuffing his mouth. Smiling, I picked up my glass.

"What's that?" he asked me.

"Wine."

"I want some," he said.

My mother said alcohol was the devil's drink. My father always gave me alcohol when I was young. He wanted all the novelty to have worn off by the time I was an adult.

I handed him the glass. "Here, take just a sip. Hold it carefully. We don't want Jerry to fall and break."

He looked at the glass. "Jerry? You've got names for your glasses?"

"Just this one," I said. "It was a gift from a friend I loved very much."

"And his name was Jerry?"

"Nope. Michael."

He looked at me, confused.

"Jerry rhymes with sherry."

He laughed and put Jerry to his lips. He tilted his head back, and before I knew it he had finished the entire glass.

"Herh!" I cried, and snatched the glass from him.

He smiled mischievously. "Sometimes I drink Daddy's beer and let him think it's Junior. So he never believes Junior when he says he doesn't drink."

I laughed. "I wish I had siblings so I could have done that."

He looked up at me and smiled. "I'm happy you came here," he said. Then he added, "I'll like to take you somewhere special tomorrow."

"Where?"

"There's this special place I know. It's a little cave, actually. Down on the beach."

"Is your father going to agree?"

Mischief glowed in his eyes. "He won't know anything about it."

I raised my eyebrows.

"Everyone is going out tomorrow. They're going to Kakum. Their church is organizing a trip there."

After the past few days, I was beginning to hate the inside of my house. Besides, I loved the sea. And I liked Wolf.

"It's really peaceful in the cave. I go there sometimes to be alone and read."

I didn't need that much convincing. "Okay. Let's do it," I said. "I'll make sandwiches for us to take along."

"Bring that as well," he said pointing to the bottle of wine on the counter.

"Oh, get away," I laughed.

I was in the kitchen making the tuna sandwiches when Wolf came over the next day.

"They've left," he said.

"Wonderful. The taxi should be here in about fifteen minutes. What did you bring along?"

He placed his backpack on the counter and opened it. I put down the knife and the loaf of brown bread I was holding and looked inside. "Nietzsche, Marx, *The State and Revolution* by

Vladimir Lenin, *Hitler: A Biography.* Why are you reading about Hitler?"

He grinned. "For when I take over the world."

"And there's a Bible in here. I thought religion was the opiate of the masses," I said with a chuckle, and returned to slicing the bread.

"I have found it surprisingly interesting. Have you read it?"

"Bits and pieces. You know, in church and stuff."

"Okay. Well, I've been reading Ecclesiastes and . . . "

"And?"

"There's something about it. I can't put it down. It has got a hold of my soul."

"Well, it was written by the wisest man who ever lived," I said.

"Up until the ninth of August 1988," he said with a grin.

I laughed and shook my head. "So tell me, how does one reconcile Hitler with Ecclesiastes?"

"Religion has always been a convenient pretext for hate and greed and lust for power. I hope to discover how people used it to gain power over the sheep. I've got to learn from my predecessors."

"And why do you want to be another Hitler or Stalin?"

He frowned. "I don't. 'Aus so krummen Holze, als woraus der Mensch gemacht ist, kann nichts ganz Gerades gezimmert werden.'"

"Huh?"

"'Out of the crooked timber of humanity, no straight thing was ever made.' Kant. Hitler and Stalin and other almost intelligent people all had ideals they wanted to build. And whenever imperfect humans want to build something perfect, wars and genocides and stuff happen. So I'll do the opposite. I'll tear down everything. You can't have war and genocides if everyone is dead."

Chuckling, I put the sandwiches into a basket and fetched two bottles of orange juice from the fridge.

Wolf looked at me and pouted.

"Yes, juice. Today is a good day." I pulled out *The Bell Jar.* "I'm taking this to read."

He took it from me. "Wasn't this written by that poet who stuck her head in her oven?"

I shrugged. "A dear old friend gave it to me ages ago, and I never bothered to read it."

We heard the sound of an approaching vehicle.

"That must be the taxi," I said. "Let's go."

In Cape Coast, nowhere is far from anywhere else, so in just a few minutes the quiet of West End Ridge and then the slow-paced hustle and bustle of the center of town were replaced by the calming murmur of the sea.

"The cave's this way," said Wolf, tugging on my coverup, and we started across the sand.

Unsurprisingly, the beach was filled with people having fun and unwinding after the stressful week.

I regretted wearing a coverup over my bikini top and shorts. The sun was the perfect height in the sky to warm my skin without scorching it.

"Hold on, Wolf," I said. I took off my slippers so I could feel the sand beneath my feet.

The mass of beachgoers and revelers thinned out gradually as we moved along the beach. Eventually the sand gave way to pale yellow rocks, and we had to scale a few large boulders to access a small cove.

"Wow," I said.

We walked over the sand to the cave entrance. It was small but perfect to sit in and watch the sea.

I set down the basket inside and spread out the mat. Surprisingly, it wasn't damp. The sand was dry and pleasant.

"Do you like it?" he asked.

"It's perfect, Wolf. It's so beautiful. Look at the rocks." I ran my hands over the black rocks arching up overhead.

"These are the rocks that remained," he said.

I glanced at him. "What do you mean?"

"Differential erosion," he said. "All the soft and weak rocks were eroded away by the sea. And only these basalts remained."

"That's interesting."

"It's kind of like life, don't you think?" he said. "Only the strong remain."

"It's exactly like life," I replied, settling down on the mat. "You think your foundations are rock solid, and then, all of a sudden, it shifts like sand beneath your feet. Even the strong fall eventually. One by one. One day even these rocks will be gone."

I immediately wished I had not said that. A darkness came over his face, and he sat down in the sand and leaned against the wall of the cave. He took out *The State and Revolution* and opened it before him, but his eyes seemed to be staring through the pages.

I picked up my novel, but before long the coolness of the cave and the peaceful drone of the waves seduced me into a sweet slumber.

Waking up was equally gentle and pleasurable. My senses returned one by one, the feel of the mat under my skin, the sound of the waves, and then finally the image of Wolf sitting by my side eating a sandwich.

"You snore terribly," he said with a smile.

I smiled back.

He popped the last bit of the sandwich into his mouth and swallowed. "That was the last one. Sorry."

I sat up. "What? Wolf, I made eight. You ate them all?"

A look into the basket revealed that was very much the case.

"I'm sorry," he said again. "They were delicious and I was hungry."

"Oh, don't worry. I was just surprised you could eat that much." I lay back down and took a sip from my water bottle. "I'm sure you must be absolutely full now."

He shook his head.

"What?"

"I didn't eat this morning," he said.

"Neither did I. Anyway, you're a growing boy." I reached out and rubbed his cheek.

He smiled. "Wolf cub, you mean."

"You know what?" I said, rising to my feet this time. "There were some guys selling kebabs near the road. I'll go buy some. I think I might also be hungry soon."

He gave me a thumbs-up sign.

The deceptive coolness of the cave made me leave my coverup behind. The sun burned my skin. I hurried over the hot sand.

I was on my way back with four kebabs when I heard an unfortunately familiar voice call, "Ahɔɔfɛ!"

A quick glance to my left confirmed it was indeed Gerald.

"Gerald, please no," I said with an outstretched hand. I quickened my steps.

He stepped in front of me and grabbed my wrists. He pulled me towards him, pressing his scrawny body against mine.

"Come on, sweetie. Of late you've not been minding me."

He then stretched his neck and took a bite out of one of the kebabs.

"Let me go, Gerald, you fool." I stamped on his foot as hard as I could.

He released my wrists and laughed, chewing like a ruminant.

"Oh, sweetie. Why the need for insults? I'm just playing with you." He then bit his lip. "You're looking great, though. You've got the body of a twenty-year-old, you know?"

"No, Gerald. I'm not your sweetie. Don't call me that. It's not just play. I'm tired. I'm tired of you and your harassment. I don't want you near me again. I don't like you, Gerald. I really don't. In fact, don't even talk to me anymore when you see me." With that, I started off.

"You're so too known. You really have a problem with your attitude," he called after me.

Incredulous, I turned. "You're insane, Gerald."

"You de bore me saf," he said. "You figure say you better pass we all or what? Why, you be gold? Commot for there. I go show you. You go regret paah. I know who you are, ashawo girl."

I threw the kebab he had taken a bite of into the sand and stormed off.

Back at the cave, Wolf stood waiting at the entrance. I handed him the three remaining kebabs.

"I stood on the rocks and I saw some guy bothering you. What happened? What did he want?" he asked.

I lay down flat on my back and massaged my wrists. Gerald's barbarous grip still hurt. Feeling too exhausted and angry to control my words, I replied, "What they always want."

Wolf sat down in the sand beside me and folded his legs. I took another swig from my water bottle.

"This must be cold comfort, but I hear men are visual creatures. And you are quite impressive visually, I think," he said, and he scratched his head. "You are, right?"

The candidness in his eyes washed all my anger away.

"I certainly hope so," I laughed.

"Are you familiar with herring gulls?"

"What are they? Some kind of bird?"

"Yes. They've got a little red spot on their bill." He touched his nose. "Well, there was this Dutch scientist, Niko something. He realized that newly hatched herring gulls received food from their parents only after they pecked at the red spot on their parents' bills."

"Okay."

"Here's the interesting part. When he replaced the parents with a wooden stick with a red stripe on it, the baby herring gulls tapped at it anyway. And when he increased the number of stripes, the baby herring gulls tapped more and harder. The larger and more exaggerated the stripe, the stronger the response."

"Uh-huh."

"And apparently there's a neural circuit in babies' brains designed to strengthen the bond between mother and child during breastfeeding. I have a hunch that part of men's brains doesn't wither away with age. Hence their fascination with those things. And also, by my estimations you must be a full C cup. Or more likely a D. Maybe 36D. I'm sure you can see what I'm getting at."

"Men like busty women?"

"Apparently. It's supernormal stimuli. The bigger, the better."

"Ei Wolf!" I clapped my hands together, laughing.

"We can illustrate this further. What's your waist size?"

"Erm, thirty. It used to be twenty-eight but I've put on a bit of weight lately."

"And your hips?"

"Forty-eight."

He then brought out a little notebook and a pencil and started to do some long division. After a few seconds, he announced the results: "0.625." He whistled. "That certainly backs it up."

I sat up. "Backs what up?"

"Women with a waist to hip ratio of around 0.7 to 0.8, especially in Africa, are consistently rated as more attractive by men, and women. Apparently a narrow waist and wide hips are subconsciously associated with fertility or something like that. You take curviness to a new level with a 0.6." He dropped the notebook and pencil back into his bag and delivered his conclusion.

"So what I'm trying to say is that unfortunately, men find you attractive."

I almost laughed. "Who wants to be unattractive?"

"Well, in our society, men are expected to do the dirty work of chasing the female. So it stands to reason that out of the universal set of available males who are attracted to you"—he bent over and drew a Venn diagram in the sand—"the ones who are likely to stop you in the street are the ones more interested in your superficial characteristics, whether they are aware of it or not. That's subset A." He pointed to the second set. "Guys in subset B will approach you much less often because physical attraction isn't that big a deal to them. Therefore the overwhelming majority of guys who will stop you in the street are basically just dogs. You'll have to sift through a lot of hay to find the needle of true love. You've been cursed with beauty and sex appeal."

"Hmm . . ."

Then he added, "Although I should make it clear that my hormones haven't kicked in yet, so I don't quite understand the mechanics of attraction. It's all conjecture at this point. And also in my opinion, biology is a *kleine Wissenschaft*, a small science."

It was hard not to smile. "You'll be an adolescent soon, and you'll understand."

"Ugh. 'Adolescence' is the most disgusting word ever."

"Oh, why?"

"Because one's thought processes becomes diluted. It's the first death of an individual, I think. After that, one is just a hormonal, sex-obsessed half brain."

After that he sighed and sulked.

"You really are serious, aren't you?" I asked him.

"I think I have three years, max, of immunity left," he said. "Then I shall become one of the dogs who torment your life so."

I sat up and placed a hand on his shoulder. "Oh, my dear Wolf, you certainly shall not."

"It's probably too late for me. I think the idea that you are basically just a, er, a v-word that cooks and cleans, has been socialized deep in my brain. It's probably lying dormant right now, waiting to reveal itself. See why I said it was a mistake on God's part to make me male? I don't like what I have to become."

"Oh, Wolf," I said with a smile. "You talk as if women are angels. But your gender does not define who you will be. You have the final say on that."

He tilted his head and his eyebrows furrowed. After a few moments of silence, he said in almost a whisper, "Does Junior belong to set A or B?"

I lay on my back, put my water bottle to my lips, and mulled it over for a long time.

10

I WAS STILL THINKING ABOUT JUNIOR THE NEXT morning as I tried to pack the empty bottles hanging around my living room into polythene bags. I had to double up the bags because they kept on tearing. I sighed. It certainly would have been much more convenient if wine came in paper cartons.

I went out onto my porch and found a rectangular parcel wrapped in brown paper. When I tore the wrappings away, I gasped.

It was a lovely charcoal drawing of me in an ornate wooden frame. And at the bottom, signed in beautiful cursive handwriting, was "S. Ofori Jnr." I stared at it for a while, transfixed.

I heard the crunching of gravel and looked up to find the devil himself approaching my porch. He wore a white shirt with a black bowtie, suspenders, black trousers, and shoes polished properly enough for me to make out my silhouette in.

"You look fancy today," I said, opening the gate for him.

"Thank you," he said with a smile. That was all he said, but he continued staring at me with the smile and a slightly lost expression.

"I got your gift, the drawing," I said.

He seemed to snap back to reality. "Oh yes, that. It pales in comparison to the real you. Anyway, I planned to hide behind your porch wall and surprise you when you came out."

I laughed.

"Ei, was there a party?" My eyes followed his to the black polythene bags at my feet.

My laughter faded to a smile.

"Anyway I thought you would find it creepy," he continued. "So I just watched from my house."

My smile widened. "Maybe I would have found it cute and romantic."

"Then give me a moment," he said, and pretended to scale the wall.

I laughed some more. "You're silly papa. Would you like to come in?"

He lengthened and loosened his shirt sleeves, which had ridden up his arms. "Actually, I was wondering if you'll go to church. With me, that is."

"Oh." I hadn't linked his fancy attire with the day being a Sunday. "Erm, I would have loved to. But I didn't plan for it, and I have things to do around the house. You know, washing and stuff."

"Okay."

"Maybe next week I'll go with you."

He gave me a thumbs-up sign. "I'll see you later then."

"Wait, before you go, I was wondering something."

"Yes?"

The words I really wanted to say wouldn't come, so instead I asked, "How did you draw me? I don't recall sitting for you or giving you my picture."

He fixed those enchanting light brown eyes on me and grinned. "Remember when you came to my studio?"

I nodded.

"I started drawing then."

"Oh, okay."

"And I finished the rest from memory."

"Esabo diɛŋtsɛ!"

He laughed. "I beg, it's all truth," he said as he walked backwards away from me.

I decided to go for it. "Your dance classes are on weekend nights, right?"

He stopped moving backwards. "Yeah."

"Including Sundays?"

He nodded. "Uh-huh."

"Well, I like to dance, you know?"

"Oh really? I thought you weren't much of a dancer."

I grinned. "Well, we'll know for sure if we go tonight."

He scratched his head. "So we should go, then?"

I chuckled. "Yes, Junior," I said. "Let's go."

He smiled. "So just to be clear, it's like a date right?"

I laughed. "No, it's not like a date, Junior. It is a date."

I spent the rest of the day lazing about in my nightie. I hadn't even showered or ironed when Junior showed up at exactly seven o'clock.

The dance classes were held at a little spot in Fourth Ridge. We entered through a little vine-covered wrought-iron gate hidden away by neatly kept bushes. It felt like being transported to another world. The sky was clear, the stars were out, the wine was sweet, the band was brilliant, and Junior was graceful and gentle.

When I woke up the following day, I was sure I was in love. The headache I had didn't bother me. I didn't even take offense when Gerald joked to Baiden that I looked average height when standing but seemed tall when I was sitting. I just sat at my desk, sipped from my water bottle, and laughed along with them.

When I got home, Junior was on my porch with a bunch of bright purple flowers. "These are for you," he said with a smile.

Wolf sighed and shook his head.

"Are you stalking me?" I asked, taking the flowers from him. I sniffed them.

"Hoh," he said. "African flowers have no scent."

I laughed. "What are these, anyway?"

He scratched his head. "I'm not quite sure. I think they are carnations. I saw them beside a road in Second Ridge."

I shook my head. "I don't think these are carnations. Maybe they are anemones."

"Rhododendrons. That's what they are," said Wolf. "Common rhododendrons."

"Whatever they are, they are an expression of affection."

Wolf made a face and declared he was off to do something worthwhile.

"How was your day?" Junior asked as I unlocked my door.

"Great. And yours?"

"It was good. I finished a piece I had been working on for a while now. I'm getting ready for an exhibition."

"That's wonderful." I pushed the door open. "Come in and make yourself comfortable."

"Actually, I can't right now," he said, standing in the doorway. "I have to go. But why don't we have dinner tonight?"

I must have given him a look because he quickly added, "Oh no, not at my place. Anywhere but there."

"Okay."

"It's another date, then. But after what happened last night, I'll have to keep you away from the wine, though."

I tilted my head. "Why? What happened?"

He smiled. "You don't remember?"

"Honestly, no. I think I may have had a little too much to drink."

His smile turned into a laugh. "A little too much?"

Now I was worried I had done something really stupid. "I hope I didn't vomit on someone," I said.

He shook his head, clearly enjoying the suspense. "If you can't remember, then don't worry about it."

"No, tell me, Junior."

He backed away from the door. "Don't worry, Desire. I'll come around later so we go."

I followed him onto the porch. "Come on, Junior, tell me. You can't just leave me hanging."

He shook his head and laughed.

"Oh, tell me la," I begged.

He just continued laughing as he opened the porch gate and stepped out.

I attempted to follow him, but the sharp little pieces of gravel on the ground hurt my bare feet.

He stuck out his tongue and then said, "Go back home, Desire."

I promised to get him back and then went back in.

It was at dinner that night that Junior finally told me how he felt. He said that he was looking to settle down and he could see a future with me. I told him I could see a future with him too.

When we were just about to board a taxi home, I realized I had forgotten my purse. We dashed back inside, and my heart leapt with joy when he told the manager that his girlfriend had left her purse behind.

That night was also when we first kissed. There was an awkward silence when he returned me home. I couldn't see his expression in the near pitch darkness. But I could tell from his body language that he was nervous. So I kissed him and wished him goodnight. Of course I didn't sleep.

The next day, Wolf again singlehandedly advanced Lighthouse Academy to the quarter finals, picking up 26,500 of the school's 27,000 points. It felt inevitable that we would win the competition. The question on everyone's lips was whether Wolf would be able to get a perfect score.

As we walked home afterwards, I told to him that Junior was now my boyfriend.

"Ew," he replied.

And I laughed.

He frowned. "I still don't think you and Junior will work out. You're too different."

"Well, I'm hopeful. I have come to love your brother. I think."

"Then you should have just remained friends with him."

"Ah why?"

"Romantic attraction is adulterated."

"Oh really?"

"It's tainted with sexual attraction. Real love inspires the mind and soul. Real love is platonic."

"So I should just remain friends with Junior, eh?"

"If you want your love to be pure and to last."

I chuckled. "You're so funny. You'll grow and understand love soon."

"Over my dead body. Romantic attachment is nothing but a can of worms, as you'll find out soon enough."

"What do you mean?"

"You're like me and he's like them," he said.

I shook my head. "Junior is actually different from most guys I've met."

All he said in reply was, "Time will tell."

Junior certainly was different. On our third date, we visited an art gallery in Pedu. After that we had dinner and enjoyed some live band music. All the while, he asked me about my life and family and listened. His hands never strayed.

On the fourth, we ate banku during my lunch break at some chop bar hidden in some corner at Kotokuraba. It was there that he suggested a trip to Accra to visit my mother. I told him she would be so overjoyed, she might just collapse.

The fifth was a trip to the beach at night that Sunday. It was actually Wolf who gave us the idea. We were going to go dancing again. But Wolf looked at us, dressed and ready to go, and said, "A walk along the beach would be much better."

Junior then looked at me and said, "That's actually a good idea. Would you like it?"

I nodded enthusiastically. But before we left, Wolf whispered into my ear, "Just don't take him to the cave. It's for us only."

The full moon shone bright in the sky, illuminating the waves as they crashed onto the shore with a steady roar. The beach was pleasant enough during the day, but I loved the intimacy the darkness brought.

I took his hand as we made our way across the soft, dry sand to the shore, where the wet sand was firmer. For a while we stood watching the expanse of the ocean while the sea breeze swept past us.

"Can you see those?" Junior asked, pointing.

I squinted. There were points of light on the horizon, a row of them.

"Yeah," I said. "What are they?"

"Fishermen."

"I can never see myself in a canoe on the open sea at night."

He chuckled. "Think about why they do it though. It's love, isn't it? They do it so their families can eat. And so the children can go to school and have a better life. That's how far love can push people." He took my hand. "Come, let's walk."

I took off my slippers. He did the same with his shoes, and we continued together.

"Junior," I said after a period of silence.

"What is it, my love?" he replied.

"Wolf told me you had an ex, a girlfriend."

He nodded. "Ah, yes. Becky."

"What happened to her? Wolf said that she . . . "

"Killed herself? Yeah. She scribbled a suicide note, locked herself in her room, and drank a bottle of disinfectant."

"That's sad."

"Yeah. It devastated me. We rushed Becky to the hospital. They tried to pump her stomach, but it was too late. They tried everything, but they just couldn't save her. I gave up medical practice after that."

I rubbed his arm. "I'm sorry."

"She said something in her suicide note. It was just rambling mostly, but something stood out to me. She said, 'The strong do what they can, and the weak suffer what they must.'"

"It kind of sounds like something Wolf would say."

"Yeah," he said. "It does. Actually, she and Kwabena were quite close. She couldn't stand him at first. I remember she refused to come to the house for like two months because she really didn't like him. She said there was something devilish about him. But they seemed to bond all of a sudden. It was weird. I was even almost jealous."

"Do you know why she did it, Junior?"

He shrugged his shoulders. "I've wondered and wondered. She seemed perfectly fine, a bit aloof, but fine."

He pocketed his hands and looked out to sea, lost in his thoughts. A cold wind blew, and I wrapped my arms around myself.

"We should have brought some wine," I said.

That brought him back. "Oh no, not after what happened the other time."

I grabbed his arm. "Yes, tell me. I want to know."

"You really want to know what happened?"

"Of course, I do. I'm curious."

"Okay," he said. "You asked for it. So by the time we got back to your place you were completely drunk—"

"I would say tipsy."

"Oh no, you were drunk papa. You had so much to drink. I have never seen a human being take so much alcohol before. Anyway, you were saying things you didn't mean. You asked me to . . ."

"To what?"

He glanced around and whispered, "To make love to you."

I burst out laughing. "Oh my, really?"

"Yes! That's not even how you said it sef."

"How did I say it?"

He smiled shyly. "You really don't want to hear that. I can't even repeat it."

"Why not? My longing been exposed already."

"It's quite vulgar," he said, and laughed. "I had no idea you had such thoughts inside your head. And you were so insistent about it."

I started to laugh again.

"I was so shocked because you seem to me to be, erm, pure and untouched by the world. I'm not sure if I'm expressing myself properly. Are you embarrassed?"

I shook my head. "No, not really. It's normal. I'm a woman, after all. And women are humans. And lust is a human thing, isn't it?"

"I just imagined that you didn't care about such earthly and vulgar things." He made air quotes around "earthly" and "vulgar."

That sent me into more fits of laughter. I snorted and that just made me laugh harder. My ribs began to hurt.

"So you care about such things?" Junior asked.

"No, it's not that. I'm just laughing because people have always associated me with"—I copied his air quotes—"the 'vulgar.' My primary six teacher, Mr. Obeng, called me a Jezebel temptress the first day he laid eyes on me. I was eleven. Imagine my confusion."

THE WOLF AT NUMBER 4

"Oh. That's not nice."

"And in my first year in Achimota, my headmistress said it wouldn't be too long before I got pregnant and dropped out. Because I was always seen walking with boys. She said in one term alone, she had seen me hold the hand of every boy in the school. They were just my friends, of course."

"They just misunderstood your gaiety and liveliness of spirit," he said.

That made me smile. "'Gaiety and liveliness of spirit.' You're beginning to sound all poetic."

"I feel poetic, Desire. That's how you make me feel. You make me want to draw roses and write lines and lines of Shakespearean sonnets."

"Aww, that's sweet, Junior."

He paused for a while and looked upwards in thought. "I think I've got it now. You're in the clouds. You aren't bothered by the world and the nitty-gritty of existence. When I'm with you, I feel like the world around me doesn't exist. You're not a common kind of girl."

"You're not exactly a common kind of guy either, you know. Some guys I know would have happily given in to my wishes."

"Those weren't your wishes," he replied. "They were the alcohol's."

He took my hand and turned to face me. He raised my chin gently as though he wanted to kiss me but instead he just stared into my eyes. After a while I began to feel self-conscious.

"What is it?" I asked.

"I can imagine spending the rest of my life with you."

My heart started to race. "Really?"

He nodded slowly. "Yes," he said. "This is unplanned, but will you marry me, Desire Mensah? I would really like you to say yes."

11

"HELLO, MA?"

Her voice was gruff. "Desire?"

"Yes, Ma."

"It's 3 a.m. What's wrong?"

"I'm engaged."

There was no response.

"To Junior."

Still, she remained silent.

"Ah, Ma, won't you say anything?

"Jeff is coming to see you."

I kissed my teeth.

"He's out of the country at the moment, but he's coming to visit you next weekend. He wanted to surprise you."

"I care nothing for Jeff. Tell him it's too late. I'm taken."

"Yoo. I just hope you've made the right decision this time. I know you and I know I can't change your mind. Only your father could. I just hope—"

"You'll see, Ma. We'll come and visit you and you'll see what a gentleman he is. He's not like the other guys before. You'll see."

12

I SLEPT LESS THAN THREE HOURS THAT NIGHT, BUT I sprang out of bed the next morning with a zest for life that only newfound love can bring. It's true what they say about you not noticing the songs of the birds and the smell of the flowers and all that until you are in love. And everywhere there was love. A couple of bees danced around a pink flower. A mother tied her son's shoelace and sent him on his way. A male dog wagged its tail and trotted after the female. Okay, maybe not that kind of love. But the world was different to my eyes that morning.

Gerald was sitting at his desk when I entered the staff common room.

"Hello, Gerald," I said, with a smile and a wave.

His head dropped and he started to leaf through some books on his table.

I shrugged and took my seat.

A few minutes later, a small head popped into the room.

"Hello, Juliet," I said, giving her an inviting smile. "Don't be scared. Come in."

The girl moved hesitantly towards my desk with that wide-eyed look of a shy child.

I enveloped her in a hug. "Who are you looking for?"

"You," she whispered.

"Me? Why?"

"Headmistress said I should call you."

I thanked Juliet and sent her off to play. Nothing was going to spoil my day, so I made a joke about going to the lion's den and strolled confidently to Madam Fire-Eater's office. I knocked and her voice came through the door, asking me to come in.

She was seated at her desk, flanked by a couple of men. Mr. Gyamfi leaned against the wall beside the door. There was a file open in front of her.

"Have a seat, Miss Mensah. This is Mr. Sawyer and Mr. Baffour. They are on the school board. And you know Mr. Gyamfi, our HR, already."

I greeted them all and reluctantly took the seat I was offered. Suddenly the office really felt like a lion's den.

Madam Fire-Eater spoke. "I'm sure you're wondering why you're here."

I nodded. My throat had gone too dry for my voice to be reliable.

"I'll go straight to the point. There have been some very serious allegations made against you, Miss Mensah. Not only that, some rumors have spread."

"Wha—" I cleared my throat. "What? What allegations? What rumors?"

Mr. Gyamfi took over. "That you exchanged sexual favors to get your job."

I jumped up. "What? Who said that?"

"Be calm, Miss Mensah," said Madam Fire-Eater. "Of course, we can't tell you who made the allegations. But we're glad you see the seriousness of the matter."

"How can I be? It's all lies. I never slept with anyone."

"We'll see about that," said Madam Fire-Eater.

"You are familiar with Mr. John Larry Addison, the former headmaster?" Mr. Gyamfi asked.

"Yes, I—"

"And did you offer him sexual favors in exchange for a job?"

"That wrinkled old man? Are you serious?"

"Have you ever been to the Grand Cape Resort, Miss Mensah?" Madam Fire-Eater asked.

I froze.

"Miss Mensah?"

"Uhm, no. Maybe."

"No? Maybe?"

"Okay, I went there with Mr. Addison, but nothing happened. I could swear it. We went there after I had gotten the job."

A collective sigh went around the room. Madam Fire-Eater looked at the others, as if to say, "I told you so."

"I'm serious. Nothing happened. He said he was just going to show me around the town because I was new."

"You had a hotel room," said Madam Fire-Eater.

"He said he didn't want to drive back. I didn't sleep with him. That's the truth."

"So what happened in the room?" Mr. Gyamfi asked. "Clear that up for us."

Tears started to well up inside me. "I don't know."

"You don't know what happened?"

I shook my head.

"But you were in the same room, Miss Mensah."

"I don't know."

"Hmm," went someone.

There was silence in the room now. My head was lowered. I couldn't look anyone in the eye.

Madam Fire-Eater broke the silence. "We put these allegations to Mr. Addison, and . . . "

I raised my head slightly and caught my breath.

" . . . And he denied that he accepted any sexual favors from you prior to giving you the job."

I let out my breath, audibly.

"But he let us know that you offered sex as gratitude for the job and for the bungalow you currently reside in, which is actually for members of the board only, not common English teachers. Of course, he refused your advances, but this is a serious breach of our code of conduct, Miss Mensah." She paused for a moment and went on. "Although it is quite clear to our eyes that you were engaged in an illicit affair with Mr. Addison, we will investigate the matter thoroughly. You have been suspended indefinitely while the investigation is conducted, and you have a month to vacate the bungalow you are currently occupying. Thank you for your time and cooperation. Have a nice day, Miss Mensah."

I just sat there, too numb to move. And as the Fire-Eater closed her file and put it away, I thought I glimpsed a hint of a smile hiding in the corners of her mouth.

"You can leave now," she said.

My limbs felt like cold lead as I somehow made my way out of the office. Getting out into the open air didn't relieve the feeling of the walls closing in on me. The noose I had been fearing had finally tightened.

I hadn't gone three steps from the office door when someone tapped my shoulder. "Miss Mensah."

It was one of the school board members, the one who was introduced as Mr. Sawyer.

"Let's walk, Miss Mensah," he said. "I'm sorry for all this mess."

I had nothing to say.

"I understand your position. These are very terrible accusations that could ruin your career and reputation. And right now it looks bad. Mrs. Anaglate isn't too fond of you either. She wants you gone immediately." Then he lowered his voice. "But the situation can be salvaged."

Hope raised my eyebrows. "How?"

"As for me, I don't care whether you're innocent or not. I am a man of considerable influence. I live at Second Ridge. House number 6. Pay me a visit this evening. We'll work something out."

"What?"

"Come to my place tonight. We'll work out this problem."

I was still confused. Then I saw it, the look in his eyes. Mr. Addison had that look in his eyes when he invited me out. Gerald had it every time he looked at me. Nii had that look often, as did Jeff and Kojo and Akwasi and Senam and Jacob and Kingsley. It was an old and familiar look—the look of greed, lust, desire.

I was sick and tired of that look.

I do not remember how I made the decision to slap him. I'm not even sure that I consciously made the decision. But all the same, my open palm connected hard with his cheek, knocking him over and sending all the children playing around into gleeful raptures.

He rose to his feet and glared at me with his hand to his cheek. "You are finished," he said. "Finished."

I turned and made my way back to the staff common room. The entire room was quiet as I packed my things and walked out. No doubt they knew already.

Only Baiden came up to me. "Here, let me help," he said. He attempted to relieve me of a stack of books I was organizing on my desk.

"I don't need—"

My outstretched hand knocked over my water bottle. It hit the ground and the cover flew off.

Everyone's eyes fell on the growing red pool around the bottle.

I dropped the stack of books on my desk, picked up my water bottle, and walked out.

On the way home, I picked up a few bottles. The sun was high in the cloudless sky, but I still needed warmth.

Drenched in sweat, I started to unbutton my blouse. My hands shook while I did. I couldn't hold on any longer so I poured myself a glass. And I was midway through the third glass when through the window, I saw Junior walking up to my porch.

"Erm, I think I should come back later," Junior said when I got the door.

I grabbed his hand. "Come on, I won't bite."

I settled him on the sofa and fetched Jerry.

"I heard what happened," he said. "I left everything and came over."

"Yeah. Sad, isn't it?" I said, dropping down beside him. I took a sip.

"I heard about the rumors. So I came to find out if . . . " He looked down and fidgeted with his fingers. "You know, if . . . "

All the warmth drained from my body. "Oh Jesus! Junior, you too?"

He jumped up. "I need to know! I need to know if you're . . . you're pure. Because I did see Addison come here one Saturday."

"If I'm pure? You and purity! Is anyone pure?"

"So you did it?"

"No! Of course not."

"And I believe you. You're uncorrupted and virtuous. You aren't capable of something low like that."

"Oh, and what do you know?"

He was taken aback. "Ei, Desire."

Shame came washing over me like black, icy waves. I walked back to the table and redid the top button of my blouse. "I'm sorry," I said. "My mother really needs the money. And I have no idea what I'll do. You don't know the consequences. This is the only job I'll ever get. What will happen to my mother? And to me?"

He came over and held my shoulders. "Don't worry. We'll be married soon. I don't care what they say about you. We both know you're not that kind of woman. I'm a good artist. My work will sell soon. And I'll be able to support you and your mother. We'll get through this together."

He hugged me but I felt nothing. I placed my head over his heart, but no warmth flowed from his body to mine. Then Jeff came to mind, his arrogant gait, his arrogant smile, his condescension and his money, his mountain of old money. I stepped back from Junior and put Jerry to my lips.

13

JUNIOR STAYED WITH ME. HE SAID THERE WAS AN exhibition in a month and if he sold enough paintings, we could not only get married but relocate to Accra. He said I had a degree so it shouldn't be too hard for me to get a job. And together we could support my mother and live a comfortable and happy life.

By the time he was done, things didn't look so bad. I could even force a smile. After hearing my tummy rumble, he went back to his place to prepare something for me. He said my box of instant noodles didn't qualify as food.

My eyes fell on the telephone, and I wondered if I should call my mother. Just when I decided that I couldn't, it rang. I picked up the receiver hesitantly.

"Hello?"

"Sweetie?"

I kissed my teeth.

"Oh, sweetie, I'm sorry. I didn't know that they would—"

I slammed the receiver down and went back to my couch.

The phone rang several times as I attempted to eat the sweet potatoes Junior had fried. I wasn't hungry.

"Aren't you going to answer it?" he asked.

I shook my head.

"Couldn't it be someone important?"

I shook my head again.

Being the wonderful man he was, he let it go.

When he was about to leave, I asked him what would happen if he didn't sell enough paintings. He looked down at the floor and back at me. "I have no choice but to sell them, then."

The next morning, he brought me oats for breakfast.

"You're not going to stay with me?" I asked as he handed the bowl over.

"I've got to go and meet some people for the exhibition," he said.

"Okay."

"So I'll see you in the evening, then."

I tried to be strong. I swept, washed the dishes I hadn't touched in days, and dusted every surface I could find. I even removed the cobwebs hiding in the corners of the room. I tried to eat. But by noon I was having a drink. I cried. Then I started to pack some of my things back into my suitcases. Successful exhibition or not, I was done here.

At one o'clock, I tuned in to the quarter finals of *Wonderkids* on the radio. Wolf predictably dominated the entire thing, securing 26,500 of his team's 27,000 points. I couldn't help but smile.

When it was slightly after four, I peeked at number 4. There was no pickup in the driveway. Before I could knock on his door, he emerged.

"I saw you coming," he said.

I wrapped my arms around him. He didn't whine or complain but stood perfectly still. When I let him go, he said, "I'll get a full-body scrub when you go away."

I laughed. "Silly boy. Anyway you were great today. I listened on the radio. I'm really proud of you."

He shook his head. "It was my worst performance."

"Ah, what do you mean?"

"I had 26,500 points, the same as the last time. I stagnated. The gradient of my life should never be zero. That's unacceptable."

"Well, it's better than the 2,000 points the other school picked up."

"It's still not 30,000. Besides, that's seven meals gone this week."

"Seven meals gone? What do you mean?"

"For every 500 points lost, I lose a meal."

"What?"

"Well, Daddy says it will motivate me to be better. I have to be better. We now have only the semifinals and finals itself to get a perfect score. I really messed up."

"Wolf, are you serious?"

"Daddy says that if a man doesn't work, he doesn't eat. So if I also don't learn, then I mustn't eat. Why do you think I was so hungry when we went to the beach?" He said it with a laugh.

I put my hand over my mouth and took a step back.

"Come on, it's not that bad," Wolf said. "He spreads it out. So I get at least a meal a day. He's not a bad person."

I couldn't say anything.

"It's just the sacrifice I have to make."

"Wolf," I said finally.

"Yes?"

"Do you want to do that show?"

"I have to."

"But do you want to?"

"Of course I want to. I have always wanted to." He scratched his head. "But of what relevance is my wish, anyway? You don't do what you want, you do what you must."

"What about your happiness?"

He looked genuinely confused. "But what's the use of happiness?"

"What do you mean by 'What's the use of happiness?' Everyone wants to be happy!"

"But no one will remember your happiness when you die. It can't buy food or clothes. Happiness doesn't teach you things or win quizzes or prizes. It has no objective value."

"Why? Why do you feel you have to jump through all these hoops? That's not a healthy way to think, Wolf."

"Well, maybe from your point of view. But I want results. I care only about results. A life without achievement is not a life worth living. You see, I know my end, Desire. There's a ditch out there waiting for me. I see it every time I close my eyes. Life's like a play, you know, a great big play. The actors and setting change with time but never the plot. I want to change the plot, you see. I must change the plot. I need to change the plot. I can't afford not to."

"Why, Wolf? Why?"

His eyes went vacant again. "'These are the words of the Teacher, King David's son, who ruled in Jerusalem. "Everything is meaningless," says the Teacher, "completely meaningless!" What do people get for all their hard work under the sun? Generations come and generations go, but the earth never changes. The sun rises and the sun sets, then hurries around to rise again. The wind blows south, and then turns north. Around and around it goes, blowing in circles. Rivers run into the sea, but the sea is never full. Then the water returns again to the rivers and flows out again to the sea. Everything is wearisome beyond description. No matter how much we see, we are never satisfied. No matter how much we hear, we are not content. History merely repeats itself. It has all been done before. Nothing under the sun is truly new. Sometimes people say, 'Here is something new!' But actually it is old; nothing is ever truly new. We don't remember what happened in the past, and in future generations, no one will remember what we are doing now. I, the Teacher, was king of Israel, and I lived in Jerusalem. I devoted myself to search for understanding and to explore by wisdom everything being done under heaven. I soon discovered that God has dealt a tragic existence to the human race. I observed everything going on under the sun, and really, it is all meaningless—like chasing the wind.'"

When he was done he said, "This is the plot, you see. And if I fail, then Solomon is right. Then futility wins. Then all this is meaningless. Then entropy wins. Then there's no point to it all. Then I don't matter."

"No! You do matter. You don't need to do all this to matter. There's more to life than stupid prizes and useless accomplishments."

He frowned and his voice came out gruff. "Daddy cares about those stupid prizes and useless accomplishments."

"Well, forget your father. Your father can go to the devil for all I care. If he cared about you, he wouldn't make you do anything you don't want to. All this is silly, really. It's a sick system out there, you know? It will use you. Then it will spit you out. It doesn't love you. They don't love you. The show is stupid. The prize is stupid. People are stupid. All this is stupid." Tears started to flow. "Don't let people use you, Wolf. Don't let them use you to satisfy their selfish dreams and ambitions. They'll lie to you. They'll fill your ears with honey. Then they will take from you. And when you're all used up and spent, you'll have to pick up the pieces of your broken life all by yourself. Don't let your father use you and destroy you. I care about you, you see. I care as if you were my own. I love you, Wolf, and I want you to be happy. I love you so much."

He said nothing.

"I'm sorry," I said, wiping the tears from my cheeks. "I lost my job yesterday. I'm sorry."

He stared at me for a while with hard, emotionless eyes. Then he said, "Is it not against our wills that we become wise? I think you should go home now."

With that, he disappeared inside.

"Wolf, wait!" I cried, but he shut the door. "Wolf!" I called out again.

But there was no reply except the lock clicking, twice.

14

THAT NIGHT I CORNERED JUNIOR. HE SAT THERE quietly while I went on and on, my anger rising with each lap I made of my living room.

"It's child abuse, I tell you. It's wrong and it's evil." I stopped and placed my hands on my hips. "Say something, eh?"

Junior simply shrugged. "Wolf doesn't mind."

"What do you mean? Wolf minds! If he doesn't then he should. How can you be so unconcerned?"

"His methods didn't work out too badly with me. As much as I didn't like them, I did become a doctor. I have that to fall back on if my art doesn't go anywhere."

"So it's okay to starve him, then?"

"No, Desire, it's not. Try and calm down, please."

"You don't understand. I know what it's like, trying to live up to others' expectations and failing. He's a child and his innocence must be protected above all else. I don't want him to hurt himself. He needs to be happy."

Junior hugged me. "Don't worry. He'll be fine. He's a tough child. Besides, in two weeks the competition will be over, just two weeks."

His calming embrace kept me silent for a while. Then I said, "He's angry with me."

"Don't worry," Junior replied. "He likes you. By tomorrow he will have forgotten about the whole matter. You'll see."

He did not forget about the matter. I went over every day, and every single time, Wolf would refuse to come see me. It was not until the next Monday, six days later, that he appeared on my front porch. I had just returned from his house and had been told he didn't want to see me.

I was letting myself in when I heard his voice say, "Hello."

"Hey," I replied. "It's been awhile. I was just from your place."

He placed his chin on the top of my porch gate. His eyes looked down, avoiding my gaze. "I know."

"How did you get here so fast and without me noticing?"

"I have been irrational," he said.

It was hard to suppress a chuckle as I walked over and unlocked the gate. "Oh, Wolf, don't worry. How are you?"

"School isn't nice without you," he said, taking a few tentative steps in.

"I taught JSS, you're in primary."

"It isn't nice nevertheless. I want to spend some time with you. Is that okay?"

"Ah, of course." Now I was starting to worry. "Is there something wrong?" I squatted before him and attempted to make eye contact.

"Oh no," he said stifling a yawn. "I'm just tired, that's all. Daddy won't be back until late, so I have some time. There's some meeting going on. I think they want to make him the head of department. I heard mummy saying it on the phone."

"Oh, okay. What should we do then? Are you hungry? I can cook some noodles."

Finally he established eye contact. "Do you want to go back to the cave?"

I shook my head. "Ei, not at this time. I'll be scared."

He bobbed his head up and down lightly in acceptance.

"Erm, how about a game of Ludo?" I asked. "I bought a board on my way here from Accra, and I've had no one to play with."

A small smile crept onto one side of his mouth. "A game completely dependent on chance to make me feel better about my life. Great."

I laughed. "You can't control everything. Come in and sit while I get the board and put the noodles on the fire."

"Actually, I'm not hungry," he said. "So don't bother."

"Oh."

"If you've got more potato chips, I would like that, though."

I smiled to myself. "Sure. I have one last can in my fridge. The Ludo board is in that suitcase over there. You can bring it out while I get the chips."

When I returned from the kitchen with the can and a bottle of wine for myself, he was seated cross-legged on the carpet. I gave him the can and joined him.

"What's your favorite color?" I asked, pouring the counters and the die onto the board. "Wait, let me guess. Red?"

He smiled. "How did you know?"

"It's also my favorite color," I replied with a grin. "You take it, though. I'll go with blue."

He slid the red counters over to his corner. "Okay. You roll first."

I did and I got a six. "Wow." I rolled again. "Two six!" And again. "Three six!"

"Ah!" he exclaimed.

"Four six, five six! And a two. Wow."

"That's unfair," he grumbled.

I laughed. "Hwɛ! Some good fortune is overdue in my life right now." I took a quick gulp directly from the bottle and brought all four of my counters into play.

When I was done advancing one of them, he said. "Let's make the game more interesting. You roll a six, you take six sips of the wine. You roll a five, you take five sips. Four, you take four sips. Like that."

"Why?"

"It balances the game out. You'll think twice about rolling so many sixes."

"It does actually sound like fun," I said. "Okay."

"Great." He picked up the die and rolled.

"One!" I exclaimed and laughed.

"This game is rigged," he moaned.

As I took the die to roll, he picked up the bottle and put it to his lips.

"Herh, young man!"

"We made an agreement just right now."

"That was for me, not you."

"Come on, it's just a sip. I've got high tolerance. Don't worry."

I thought about it and shrugged.

"Thank you," he said, and took his sip, which was actually a large gulp.

I shook my head and rolled my turn. Four.

After moving my second counter four places, I swallowed four gulps. A shiver went down my spine. I smiled.

He watched me closely.

"I'm tingling," I said, and giggled.

He took the die and blew air over it. "Give me six," he whispered.

I almost rolled over with laughter. "I can't believe you of all people would do something like that."

He laughed with me. "That's how desperate I am." He threw the die down, and after bouncing around for an unusually long time, it finally settled with six dots facing upward. He punched the air in delight and rolled again, getting a five. He grabbed the bottle and began to drain it.

I snatched the bottle from him. "No, no. Don't take so much."

My roll gave me a three, but there was barely enough for a mouthful. "See what you've done?"

His mouth was still so full that he could only shrug in defense.

I made my way to the kitchen and brought out another bottle. "This is my last but one bottle. So we better use it wisely. I better take the first blow to inaugurate it."

"That's not fair."

I laughed. "Life's not fair. Let's get back to our game. One, two, three places. It's going to take a miracle for you to win this game. Your turn."

But Wolf just sat there, staring off into the distance. "I'm happy," he said.

I smiled. "Yes, wine tends to do that."

"Let me come over there," he said, crawling on all fours over to my side and snuggling up against me. "This feels so much better."

My smile widened. "Same here, Wolf. You're nice and warm."

I offered no resistance as he loosened the bottle from my grip and swallowed a hearty mouthful. He licked his lips and said, "This is all just dopamine in our reward pathways, you know. We're hijacking the brain's reward system."

"Life is hard. We've earned the reward," I said as he rolled the die and got a one.

"Hurray. Another sip for me," he said.

While he took his drink, I rolled and got a two. When he was done, he passed the bottle to me.

"But in this world the price of happiness is high," he said. "It's funny how we're drinking to be happy, but what we're actually doing is altering our brain chemistry to make us more prone to feeling bad. It's like pursuing happiness actually makes you sadder. And pursuing sadness makes you sad all the same."

"Come on, Wolf, don't be Johnny Raincloud. We're happy now. Things are looking up. I'm marrying your brother, he's going to have a great exhibition, and we'll move somewhere great. We'll become family. Oh my, I never thought of that. What do you think, Wolf? We'll be family. Things really are looking up!"

"Well . . . ," he said. "Only to come crashing back down again. Unfortunately, misery is not wine-soluble." He sighed and rolled the die. "Four. Want to know a secret?"

"Sure."

He took the bottle from me and drank his share. Then he wiped his lips with the back of his hand. "I'm tiring. I really am," he said.

Suddenly I could see it. His eyes were tired and bloodshot. His shoulders sagged and his head drooped. I felt the cold creeping in again.

"I feel the strength leaving my body. Shouldn't I be getting stronger as I grow older? It confuses me. There's a thing in my chest I can't seem to get rid of. This feminine disease . . . "

"Oh, Wolf, don't be morose," I implored. "You'll make me sad for you. Let's talk about something else. Want to know my secret?"

"Okay."

"I have lived, Wolf. I have had fun. I have done so many things, experienced, felt, sensed. Life would be so great if there weren't any consequences. I haven't done so well with consequences. Consequences ruin everything. Consequences have ruined my life. They have taken my joy. I've been robbed. I need a drink. Hand me the bottle. There's so much pleasure in the world you know. Once I—"

He sat up suddenly. "Wait! I know where it's from. We get it from our mothers. That's where the infection occurs."

"Huh? Infection?"

"Yes!" he cried. "Think about it. Men are raised by women most often. That's where we pick up these feelings and emotions and nauseating sentiments. Ugh, I hate emotions. They make you so sensitive and feely."

"I like sensitive men."

He frowned and kissed his teeth. "You like sensitive men, or men who are sensitive to your feelings? Women care nothing for our feelings."

"Ei, Wolf," I laughed.

"I'm serious," he replied.

"Yeah," I said, bringing my laughter under control. "You kind of have a point. There's a point where sensitivity becomes much less appealing. Like, I can't have you crying on my shoulders every day. What is that? If I'm the one comforting you always, who will comfort me?"

He chuckled and grew serious again. "But we can't be like you guys. It's a struggle, you know? Sometimes I feel things I shouldn't, you know? Like, they don't make sense. There's no reason why I should feel them. But I do. I think I need psychiatric help because it makes no sense."

"Here," I said, handing him the bottle. "This will fix it."

"I'm scared people will find out," he went on. "That I'm irrational sometimes. I'm really terrified. They'll think I'm crazy."

"I know what they'll do," I said. "All too well." I wiped a tear that had perched itself on the edge of my eyelid. "You've done it, Wolf. Now we're sad. Congratulations."

He laughed. "The sadness is good. Solomon said the sadness is better than happiness. How did it go? 'Sorrow is better than laughter, for sadness has a refining influence on us.' 'Sorrow is better than laughter.'" He offered me the bottle. "Here, quaff your share of this kind nepenthe."

I took it. "I'm glad you're here, though. Drinking alone is no way to drink. Believe me, I know."

"I suppose so."

I began to run my hands through his tough and spiky hair, tough and spiky, but surprisingly soft near the roots. "Oh, Wolf, oh, Wolf."

"What is it?"

"You remind me so much of my son," I whispered. "He would have been about your age by now. The truth is, I wish you were mine. Don't you wish you were mine? I would take you away from here. I would take you somewhere safe."

"Daddy would be sad, I think," he said.

"Your father, what does he know? Does your father love you more than I do?"

He shrugged. "I wouldn't know. I don't know love."

"Tell me," I said. "Where would you like us to live? I want you to come back to Accra with me. No one loves you here."

He made a sound indicating disgust. "That conformist city sickens me."

"I can see you when you're twenty-something and graduating from university. I would be so proud. And you'll have a girlfriend who loves you. And you'll propose. And you'll get married on a beach in California. And we'll live together in Barcelona. Together, just you and me. And—"

"Why were you suspended?" he asked.

"What?"

"The sheep say you were naughty with Mr. Addison."

"I wasn't!"

"Of course you weren't," he said. "I know you weren't. That's why I'm asking why they would suspend you."

"I'm glad you believe me. It's just the stupid board and that Providencia woman. She never liked me, you know. We call her Madam Fire-Eater, you know?" I giggled.

"I can get rid of people," he said softly. "I can get rid of her if you want."

I looked into his eyes. He looked straight back.

"How?" I asked.

"Lead her in to the catacombs, chain her to a wall, start laying bricks," he said with an evil grin.

I clapped my hands together, laughing. "You should really stop reading Poe. He'll give you ideas."

"Or maybe bury her beneath the floorboards," he added with a wink.

"Silly boy," I said, giving him a light shove.

"I'm glad you understand me, Desire," he said with a smile. "Everyone else—they have sticks sharpened at both ends for me. And for you too."

I planted a kiss on his forehead. "I know."

Then someone knocked on the door.

"There's someone tapping, gently rapping, rapping at your chamber door," Wolf said.

"Shhh! Don't let them hear us," I whispered.

The knocking came again.

"This is somewhat louder than before," Wolf continued. "'Let me see, then, what thereat is, and this mystery explore. Let my heart be still a moment and this mystery explore. 'Tis the wind and nothing more.'"

"Shhh!"

The door opened. I had forgotten to lock it. In came Junior's head, his beautiful head. And out of his beautiful mouth came, "Ah, Kwabena?"

"Oh, hey, Junior," I called. "Come join us."

He entered the room and surveyed all before him with a look of incredulity. "What's going on? You should be at home studying. Ma said you just walked out of the house."

"Ma has no—" He burped. "Oops."

"Wait, have you been drinking?" He turned to me. "You gave him alcohol?"

"Come on. It's just wine," I said. "It's liquid happiness. Join us and be happy. You seem so sober; try not to let anyone notice. Come, come sit by me and let me give you my happiness, my crimson happiness."

"Don't fall into her trap, Junior!" cried Wolf. "The alcohol has got to her cerebral cortex. This is how teenage pregnancies happen. Beware! Beware lest she capture you. Beware! Be—"

"Oh, shut up there," snapped Junior. "Desire, I'm shocked you would do this. And on today of all days. He has school tomorrow. The semifinal is tomorrow."

"Oh," was all I could say.

He picked Wolf up, slinging him over his shoulder. "You, your father will kill you today."

"Unhand me, rapscallion!" Wolf cried. "Let me get one last drink, please. Just a sip for the road."

"Be quiet over there," said Junior, slapping his buttocks. Without saying a word to me, he walked out.

Wolf yawned widely as his head disappeared through my door. "Oh dear, my medulla," I heard him say.

15

EVEN OVER THE RADIO, I COULD HEAR THE LETHARGY in Wolf's voice. Twice he yawned out loud. I myself had woken up that morning with a searing headache made worse by guilt.

"If I had remembered the semifinal was today, I never would have allowed him to drink with me," I told Junior.

With a hug, he eased my feelings of culpability. "He didn't seem that bad this morning," he said. "Besides, this is Kwabena we're talking about. He won the competition the very day he was born."

Junior's faith in his little brother was not misplaced. Wolf carried his team to the finals. I would have been ecstatic if he had not obtained his worst-ever score, just 15,000 points, halfway to the perfection he so desired. That brought the remorse flooding back.

A part of me was relieved, though. He didn't need that perfect score. He didn't need the scholarship. He didn't need to jump so many classes. He would still win the competition, but now he had one less chance to have his childhood stolen away from him.

He would no doubt be disappointed and hurt and even embarrassed. But that would pass. In time he would come to appreciate this stroke of good fortune, this happy accident which saved him from the world and its heartless cruelty.

When I was sure that Wolf would be home, I made my way over. It was a hot day. I hurried through the scorching sun and was relieved when I got to his shaded porch. I knocked on the front door. A few moments passed. There was no answer.

I knocked again. "Wolf?"

This time I heard movement.

When the door swung open, there stood not Wolf but Mr. Ofori.

"Come in, Miss Mensah," he said, and disappeared back inside.

I followed him in warily. The curtains were all drawn, so it took a while for my eyes to adjust to the darkness.

Mr. Ofori was by the dining table. He poured himself a glass of whiskey.

"I'm here for Wolf, for Wolfgang," I said, setting my bag down on a chair.

"Of course you are," he said almost inaudibly.

The atmosphere was stifling. It seemed hard to even breathe properly. "Is he around?"

He downed the whole glass in one gulp. "No, he is not."

I grabbed the strap of my bag. "Okay. I should go, then."

He looked at me. "Oh no. Stay, Miss Mensah. You and I have much to discuss."

"Actually, I have somewhere to—"

"I heard what you told my son last time, out there on my front porch," he said.

I froze. "I—"

"My pickup was with the mechanic, but I was in here. I heard everything. He shouldn't go on the show, eh? I'm giving him pressure, eh? I should go to the devil, eh?"

"Well, no, not exactly. He's a kid, you see. He should be happy. He should be free."

"Free?" he asked with a little laugh. He set his glass down on the table and he looked me in the eyes. "Free to be you?"

I ground my teeth.

"Yes, Mr. Ofori. Free. I'll be honest, I don't like how you treat your son. He's a human being, not a machine. You can't decide when he eats and when he doesn't. He's such a lovely child, but his mind is, is, is, overused. He pushes himself and he denies himself because he thinks that's what you want."

"That's exactly want I want! I want him to succeed. He must be great. I'm not going to have another useless layabout in my house! I will not accept it. Wolfgang Kwabena Ofori will grow and be great, and I shall be proud of him."

I picked up my bag and moved to the doorway. "I see. It's about you, then. Mr. Ofori, to be honest, I don't think you love your son at all. I think you're using him. You're a mean bully, and Wolf deserves a far better father than you."

With an impossibly fast movement, he threw the glass down onto the table, shattering it into a thousand pieces.

Before I could react to that, he slammed the door shut with one hand and shoved me against it with the other. He grabbed my face. "Look at me!"

His hands were vibrating. I did not dare resist.

"I'm a bad father, right? That's why I get him drunk the night before an important quiz, a quiz which could change his life forever. That's your way of helping him, right? Turning him into a drunk?"

His grip was so tight on my jaw that I could not even move my lips.

"I know who you are, Desire," he said. "I know who you are." He let me go.

My legs gave way beneath me and I slumped to the floor. Now tears started to well up behind my eyes, tears of disbelief and shock.

He walked over to the dining table with the broken pieces of glass crunching under his boots. I heard him pour more whiskey into another glass.

"Are you familiar with a Kwesi? Kwesi Opare?" he asked.

My blood stopped cold in my veins.

"No answer, Desire?"

"No. I don't know any Kwesi Opare," I whispered.

"Really? He seems to know you quite well. How do you kids say it nowadays? He opened your chapters?" he said with a chuckle.

I tried to get to my feet. "I'm leaving. I'm going home."

He grabbed my arm and dragged me to a chair. "You're going where? No. You're going to sit and listen."

"No, I don't want to," I protested, and tried to rise.

A slap knocked me down into the seat.

"That's better," he said. "You've had your say and now I'm going to have mine. And you're going to hear every single word. I really don't know how you expected someone like yourself could come into my home and deceive me."

"Just let me go. I don't know what you mean."

He sat down opposite me with his drink in his hand. "Oh, stop pretending, Desire. The game is up. You see, there's a guy, Nathaniel, who does some work for my consultancy firm. He's like a son to me. He spent some time in Cantonments and met Kwesi Opare. And did he have some fantastic tales to tell about you."

"No. Stop it. Please."

"Apparently you're well known in the Cantonments area. You used to live on Mokwe Street, didn't you? House number 66."

Gathering enough strength, I made for the door, but he cut me off and threw me down to the carpet. He knelt over me, both legs astride, and pinned both my hands down.

"You will listen to me! Bar kyɛnsee, they used to call you, the boys in the area. Before you claim you don't understand Twi either, it means chop bar bowl. Chop bar bowl, Miss Desire Mensah. That's what you were. That's what you are. All you needed was a bed to lay on, so you could spread your legs. Sometimes the bed wasn't even necessary, sometimes the corner behind the pharmacy was enough. And you didn't even do it the proper way. You liked unnatural things. Kwesi wasn't even surprised when you came to beg him for money to buy a pregnancy test kit. And even that, you paid back the money with your body."

He let go of my arms but continued to sit on kneel over me. I had no strength to fight. I could only cry.

"Look at you," he said. "Look at you. You walk in here, shaking your behind left and right, and you think you can deceive us. You think you can deceive me? I know who you are underneath that fake hair and those painted nails and those tight clothes you wear. I know who you are. You're a common ashawo. No amount of aburokyire manners or eating fufu with a spoon can change what you are."

"You don't understand," I managed to say through my sobs. "My father died and—"

He placed a finger over my lips. "I'm not done talking, woman. You know what Nathaniel was doing in Cantonments in the first place? Your old school, they needed my firm's expertise to expand their classroom block."

I closed my eyes. "No, not that. Of all things, not that."

"And did he hear a lot about you. It turns out you didn't leave your job. Oh no. You're running away. You were fired, sacked, disgraced. Not because of the rumors that you slept with the music teacher. Not because of the rumors about you and the bursar as well. But because of Augustine, little Augustine."

I tried to rise, but he held my hands down.

"Having an affair with a fourteen-year-old boy, a fourteen-year-old boy. For a whole year. How could you do something like that? Is that the extent of your depravity? And you stand here and act all high and mighty and pontificate and criticize me and how I treat my child?"

He brought his face close to mine. "I do not want you near my son anymore, have you heard? Who knows what you plan to do with him? What do you mean by telling him you love him? Did you carry him in your womb for nine months? You love him and yet you plan to destroy him with your corruption and debauchery."

He let go of one hand but squeezed the other. It hurt.

"You will stay away from him," he repeated.

He was so close to me and his body weighed so heavily on me that I could not utter a word or even nod. I could not even gasp or jerk when I felt movement around my lower regions.

"If you say anything," he growled in my ear, "Junior will find out what an ashawo you are. He will throw you away like the rubbish you are. Today you will learn your place."

So I remained completely silent, closed my eyes, and just sobbed.

16

I STILL LAY IN MY BATHTUB WHEN NIGHT FELL. MY
hands swept over my flesh mindlessly, as if directed by someone
else. But still the dirt remained. Two hundred baths could not
wash the dirt off my skin, much less touch that within my soul.
Not even the wine could wash away the grime and muck built
up inside me.

Rather, with every bottle I emptied, the dirt seemed to
grow and coagulate inside me, forming a wall, a wall of guilt
and shame. Soon it enclosed me, blocking everything out. There
was no light and no sound, no sensation. It was just me and the
towering barrier of the dirt of my errors.

Every now and then, the chaos of the outside world would
threaten to break through. The walls would shake and tremble.
But the wine would save me. All would grow quiet again. And
I would have some respite.

But the chaos always returned, more violent and frightening
than before. It came and went, quicker and stronger and louder,
until there was suddenly a blinding light.

I let out a shriek and dove underneath the covers.

"You wouldn't come to the door. I was worried," said a voice, Wolf's voice.

"Close the curtains!"

"Why?"

"Just close them! It's too much," I begged him.

"Okay."

Once the room was safe again, I raised my head. "How did you get in here?"

"I learned how to pick locks," he said. It was too dark to see his face, but I made out his silhouette by the window.

"I need you to leave," I said.

"Why? What's wrong, Desire?" He stepped towards me. "You've been drinking—more than usual. Your sink is choked with vomit."

"No! Don't. You shouldn't be here. Go away. It's not safe for you to be here. I'm . . . filthy."

He froze in place. "What do you mean?"

I pulled the covers over my head. "Just leave me, Wolf."

"What is it? Why don't you want to tell me?" His voice was softer now, and pleading.

"Nothing. Just go."

He was silent. He was silent for so long I began to wonder what he was doing. When I looked back over the covers, he was gone.

17

HE WAS GONE, BUT SO WAS MY FORTRESS. I BARELY made it to the bathtub to vomit. I sat on the floor, slumped against the wall. My head throbbed and my back ached. Every bottle in the house was empty.

Once darkness fell, I slipped out of my house and headed for the mart at the filling station. It was a cloudy night and all the streetlights were off, but I pulled up my hood anyway.

Number 4 was lit brightly. There were cars parked outside it, and I could hear the indistinct drone of a small crowd emanating from the inside. I hurried past it and into the shadows.

Gabriel took his sweet time bagging my strawberry wine and chocolates. He examined every single bottle even though all five of them were identical.

"You like wine paah," he said.

I bit my lip and avoided his gaze.

"A pretty girl like you shouldn't be drinking like that."

"Rather?"

There was a bottle of bleach sitting on a shelf nearby. I placed it on the counter. While he wasted time with that too, I took out my key, stuck it into the cork of one of my bottles, and twisted out the cork.

His eyebrows rose.

"Practice makes perfect."

He watched me as I held the bottle to my lips. "Everything will be one fifty thousand," he said.

I put the bottle down. While I was straightening out the notes, he said, "I would like to be your friend if you need one."

I hurried out. It didn't take me long to finish the bottle. I threw it into a nearby bush.

"That's littering."

I turned around.

"Don't run from me," said Wolf. I couldn't see his face in the darkness.

"How long have you been there?"

"I followed you the moment you left your house. You were bound to come out sooner or later."

I was silent for a while. We started to walk. "We can't be friends anymore," I said.

He said nothing in response.

"How is Junior? Does he ask of me?"

"He banged on your door every day. You screamed at him to go away. He's worried."

I sighed. "Tell him I'm sorry. Tell him I just need some time to get over some stuff. Tell him—"

"I know what stuff."

I stopped dead in my tracks.

"I know what happened."

"Nothing happened," I said. "Leave it alone."

"I looked around your house. You have a pair of blood-stained panties. And there's blood on one of your skirts."

"It could be—"

"Our carpet has stains on it. Dark stains. My father sent it to the cleaners, but I saw them as it was being rolled up."

Tears started to betray me.

"It was him, wasn't it?"

I couldn't say anything. I just tried in vain to wipe my tears.

The streetlight above us suddenly flickered on.

Wolf's face was expressionless as he surveyed mine. His eyes followed a tear as it made its way down my cheek. Then his forehead wrinkled, his eyes narrowed. His breathing sped up. His fists clenched. His chest rose and fell ever faster. The lights went back out and all I could hear was his breathing, quick and sharp. Then it stopped.

"Let's go," he said, taking my wet hand.

I cried all the way back.

When we got home, he sat me down on my bed and told me he would be back.

He returned a few minutes later with toasted bread and tea. He sat beside me and watched me eat. There was no hint of emotion in him.

When I was done, he took the plate and cup away and returned with my towel. "Here, take a warm bath," he said.

I returned to meet neatly ironed clothes on my bed. Wolf helped me get into them. After that, we sat at the dining table. He poured me a glass of wine.

For a while, there was no sound except for my intermittent sniffing and the clinking of the bottle against Jerry.

Then Wolf said, "I'm sorry."

"It's not your fault. I should have just—"

"There's something you need to do right now."

His eyes told me what he wanted from me.

"No," I said shaking my head. "I can't. I'll deal with it. This too shall—"

"It shall not pass. It would not pass. It *should* not pass. How can you just accept something like this?"

I looked away. "Nothing good ever comes out of it. Besides I don't want to lose you guys. I can deal with it. I truly can. It was kind of my fault anyway. I'll just suck it up this time."

He was angry. "There's a time to give to God and there's a time to stand up for yourself. All your life have they not ogled you, catcalled you, touched you, and taken from you? When will you put your foot down? When will you take your humanity back?"

"When the time is right, I'll do it," I said, and started to rise from the table.

He grabbed my hand. "All those who hurt you must pay."

"But—"

"They cannot destroy you. I will not allow it. Who are they to think they can just hurt you and go scot-free?"

"What if Junior—"

"Junior, my foot. You must do it, Desire, and you must do it tonight."

He filled Jerry and handed it to me. "Drink and—"

Suddenly there was a siren in the distance. Our eyes met and went to the window. Blue-and-red lights pierced the darkness as a police car came up the road. It turned towards number 4 and stopped.

"Wolf, what have you done?"

He made for the door and I hurried after him. "Wolf!"

I followed him outside and towards his house. Three policemen stood by their car. People began to emerge from the house, first Mr. Ofori's stocky figure, then his wife, several people I didn't know, Madam Fire-Eater, and then Junior. Words were exchanged, and then Mrs. Ofori placed her hands on her head while others gasped.

Wolf stopped a few meters away and I caught up to him. Everyone had their attention on the policemen, so no one noticed us out on the periphery but within earshot.

Mrs. Ofori spoke. "Are you sure you've got the right house, Mister . . . ?"

"Inspector. Inspector Blankson," said one of the policemen. "Yes. We wrote down the address we were given." He took out a sheet of paper and read from it. "Number 4, West End Ridge. This is the place, isn't it?"

"Whoever gave you that address must be mistaken," Mr. Ofori said.

"So what's going on here?" asked Inspector Blankson.

"How is that your concern? It's a party," replied Mr. Ofori.

"What party?"

Mrs. Ofori answered. "My husband is the new head of department. We're celebrating—"

"Adjoa, you will stay out of it," Mr. Ofori said. 'Look, Inspector, you're interrupting our gathering. There's no rape here, as you can see. You were clearly misled."

"We'll determine that for ourselves." Inspector Blankson turned to his colleagues. "Sakyi, Twumasi, look around the premises."

Mr. Ofori was furious. "You can't do that. Where's your warrant?" He stepped into the path of the two officers.

"Boss, please move aside," said the officer referred to as Sakyi.

"Where is your warrant?"

"Kwame, just let them search the place," said his wife. "After all, there's nothing in there."

"Adjoa, I said stay out of it. Shut up!"

Twumasi attempted to step round Mr. Ofori, but he grabbed the policeman and tried to shove him back. Junior stepped in to separate the two. The grapple swiftly descended into a melee.

By the time Sakyi and a few other people from the crowd had separated them, Junior was bleeding from the lip.

"Leave me!" cried Mr. Ofori, struggling to break free.

"If you do not calm down immediately, you will be under arrest," said Inspector Blankson coolly and without uncertainty. The threat subdued Mr. Ofori, who stopped struggling.

"Now, Twumasi, Sakyi, go search the premises," Inspector Blankson ordered.

They disappeared into the house with Mrs. Ofori close behind. "Please don't mess up the house, oh, I beg."

"See how you've disgraced yourself in front of your guests," said Inspector Blankson to Mr. Ofori.

Mr. Ofori glared at him and looked around at the shocked faces of those he had invited to celebrate his achievement. He pulled himself together and started to straighten his tie. "You people will see," he mumbled. "You don't know who I am. You don't know who my friends are."

Inspector Blankson refused to take the bait.

"Who even called you koraa?" continued Mr. Ofori.

"The caller didn't give us his name, but he was young. He sounded like a young boy," answered Inspector Blankson.

Mr. Ofori couldn't believe it. "A young boy?" Suddenly his expression changed. His eyes began to rove about. Before long, they found mine.

I took a step back. Then I saw it; he was afraid.

Just then Twumasi and Sakyi emerged from the house and shook their heads.

"Very well," said the Inspector. "It appears there's no problem here."

Twumasi and Sakyi made their way over to the police car and opened the doors.

Inspector Blankson turned to the crowd. "So we were misled? No one here has any problem?"

Bemused looks were exchanged and heads were shaken. Mr. Ofori glanced at me. I dodged his eyes. Wolf stepped on my foot.

"No one here was harassed in any way?" he asked again. Wolf pressed down harder.

Mr. Ofori seemed confident now. "Didn't I tell you?" he said with a sneer.

Inspector Blankson nodded. "Okay, then, we're—"

The words just flew out of me. "It was me."

Everyone turned, surprised to find me there. Junior's eyebrows flew up when he recognized me. My legs began to wobble. I looked down at the ground. "It w-was me," I repeated.

The inspector stepped towards me. "It was you? Someone raped you?"

I nodded.

He placed both hands on my shoulders. "Who did it?" he asked.

I raised my hand and pointed. "Him."

18

IT WAS COMPLETE CHAOS AFTER THAT.

Mr. Ofori said I was a liar and an ashawo. He had to be restrained by Sakyi and Twumasi. Mrs. Ofori just started to cry. Junior held her and avoided my gaze. His guests asked me if I was sure and what I could have done to tempt him because they knew he wasn't that kind of man.

The police escorted me home. They sat me down and asked me what happened. I told them everything. I told them I had gone over to see Wolf a few days ago but he wasn't there and Mr. Ofori had forced himself on me.

Twumasi asked me why I didn't report earlier. I told him I didn't know why. He nodded.

Sakyi asked why I wasn't crying and being all hysterical, and when I told him I was numb, he also just nodded.

It was clear they didn't believe me.

Mr. Ofori showed up and told the police that I was lying and that I was a prostitute. His wife and Junior arrived shortly after. Junior looked at the ground the entire time.

Mr. Ofori told them I was one of Addison's small girls. He told them everything about my past and Augustine. He said he even suspected that I was doing the same to Wolf, and he had warned me to stay away from him. And that all this was just me trying to spite him. He pointed to the empty bottles lying around my living room and said I was also a drunkard.

Madam Fire-Eater wormed her way into the room to add that I had used my body to get a job and that that was the kind of woman I was.

They fetched Wolf and asked him if I had ever touched him inappropriately. He shook his head firmly.

They then asked him if he was the one who called them. He nodded.

When asked how he knew what had happened, he said he had figured it all out. He said I had been acting funny and he had seen blood on my underwear and skirt and that there were dark stains on their living-room carpet. And when he asked me, I confirmed his suspicions.

At the mention of the carpet, Mrs. Ofori started to sob. Junior patted her back consolingly. He still wouldn't look at me. Wolf stretched out his hand to hold hers but she swatted it away.

I just couldn't do it. "It's a lie," I said.

There was a collective "What?"

I could hear my heart pounding in my ears. "I wasn't raped. It's a lie."

Wolf shot me a quizzical look, his eyebrows furrowed. I looked down at my feet.

"What are you saying, madam?" Inspector Blankson asked.

"Everything is a lie. I made it up."

"I told you!" shouted Mr. Ofori. "I told you she's a liar."

"I'm not surprised," said Madam Fire-Eater.

Inspector Blankson grabbed my hand and made me look in his eyes. "Look, madam, we don't have time for games. Rape is a serious accusation. Tell us the truth."

"We had an argument and I wanted to spite him," I said with a calmness I didn't know I had.

"What about the stains the boy mentioned?" He pointed to Wolf. "I'd like to see the carpet. Sakyi, Twumasi, did you notice any stains on the carpet?"

They both shook their heads.

"I took it to the cleaners," said Mr. Ofori. "I cut myself on a piece of broken glass." He turned to his wife. "You see, I showed you the glass that broke?" She paid no heed to him and continued sobbing. He turned back to the inspector and added, "The blood stained the carpet. That's probably what my son saw and was confused."

"Hmm . . . What about the underwear?"

"Do you really need to ask me this question?" I said. "Besides, I washed it a long time ago."

Wolf shook his head. "I don't understand why—"

"Hey, shut up!" snapped his father. "What do you know? Go home and go and wait for me. Today you are finished."

Wolf made his way to the door, and Inspector Blankson turned to me. "I don't know what is going on here, but we have only your word to go on here. If you say there wasn't any rape, then we're all going to go home."

"Don't worry, Inspector. Goodnight, sir."

"Yoo," said the inspector. He put on his cap. "Sakyi, Twumasi, yɛnkɔ."

Mrs. Ofori was still sobbing into Junior's shirt as everyone filed out of my living room. And Mr. Ofori was still telling everyone what a prostitute I was. I followed till I reached my porch gate.

"You better change," Inspector Blankson said to me as he entered the police car. "Your lifestyle won't help you."

Mr. Ofori grabbed Wolf's ear and began to twist it. As their family started off into the darkness, only Wolf turned to look at me. His look of fear and confusion shattered the dam walls, and tears started to stream down my face. I placed my hand over my mouth and wondered what I had done.

The moment the blue-and-red lights of the police car were swallowed by the night, the howls started. The wind carried Wolf's cries of pain straight into my heart. Each lash and each blow seemed to reverberate in my bones. No mercy was being shown. Even the screams of his wife and first son did not lessen the venom in his father's blows.

When I saw their door open and Wolf emerge, I ran out to meet him. His father stomped after him, sleeves rolled up, sweat dripping from his face, and belt in hand.

"YOU BETTER COME BACK HERE, YOUNG MAN," roared his father.

Wolf stopped midway between me and his father. Stanley Ofori glared at me.

"YOU BETTER COME BACK HERE OR YOU ARE DEAD."

Wolf glanced at me, then his father. He turned to face him.

"I SAID GET BACK HERE NOW."

Slowly he took a step back.

"KWABENA, I AM GIVING YOU FIVE SECONDS TO GET BACK HERE."

He took another step back.

"FIVE."

Another step.

"FOUR."

Another step.

"THREE."

Yet another step.

"TWO."

He was almost within reach now.

"ONE."

Wolf took one last step back, and finally I wrapped my arms around him and kissed his head. "I'm so sorry, Wolf. I'm so sorry."

"I see," said Mr. Ofori. "Do not ever come back to my house."

19

I HAD BEEN LASHED ONLY ONCE IN MY LIFE. IT WAS the only time my father ever lost his temper with me. Jason and I had snuck out to the disco one night. Jason was twenty-four and I was seventeen but I looked twenty-one, so we were allowed in without any problems. Jason was okay, but he wasn't really my type. But he smoked and was cool and had a nice car and knew all the fun places in town, so I hung around him and he got to tell everyone I was his girlfriend.

When he brought me home that night, my father and mother were sitting on the front porch waiting. I knew I was in big trouble, but I didn't want Jason to think I was scared, so I allowed him to kiss me goodnight. He waved goodbye to my flabbergasted parents as he drove off, leaving the smell of exhaust and cigarettes in his wake.

The welts all over Wolf's back were just like the ones I got from my father's belt that night. He remained impassive as I applied an ice pack to his bruises and apologized to no end. He did not whimper and no tears formed in his eyes. He just sat there.

After a while I got him two tablets of paracetamol. "That's 1000 grams," he finally said. "The recommended dosage for children under twelve is 480 to 500 grams."

I knelt before him, gave him a glass of water, and placed a hand lightly around his neck. "Just take it. The pain will go away faster."

After a moment of hesitation he swallowed them in a single gulp.

I rested his head gently against my chest. "I'm sorry," I whispered.

"Do you think I'm angry with you?" he mumbled, repositioning his head and drawing closer to me.

"I'm afraid you hate me."

"I'm just confused."

"I was going to destroy your family. I couldn't bring myself to do that."

"Things didn't just go according to plan."

"I told you. They rarely do."

"I'm really confused. I'm not sure that was correct procedure." I smiled.

He fell silent for a while and then asked, "Will you still marry Junior?"

I had completely forgotten that I was engaged. "Uhm, sure. He loves me and I love him. Nothing has changed, really. Marrying Junior will be good for me. He'll help me take care of my mother."

"Okay." He pulled away from me. "I think I should try to sleep as the painkillers kick in. I'll need to be up early tomorrow."

"Sure. Would you mind sharing my bed with me? It's wide enough for two."

He had no objections, so I went into the bedroom and smoothed my bedsheets and replaced the pillowcase I had not washed in God knows how long.

"Do you prefer the lights on or off?"

"Off. It's safer," he said.

So I turned off the lights and lay down beside him, confident I would not sleep although I was exhausted.

After what felt like an hour, I found myself beginning to drift off when I heard Wolf singing softly but clearly. He sang the slow and haunting song over and over again until he fell asleep.

If you want to find the Sergeant,

I know where he is, I know where he is, I know where he is.

If you want to find the Sergeant, I know where he is,

He's lying on the canteen floor.

I've seen him, I've seen him, lying on the canteen floor,

I've seen him, lying on the canteen floor.

If you want to find the Quarter-bloke,

I know where he is, I know where he is, I know where he is.

If you want to find the Quarter-bloke, I know where he is,

He's miles and miles behind the line.

I've seen him, I've seen him, miles and miles and miles behind the line.

I've seen him, miles and miles and miles behind the line.

If you want to find the old battalion,

I know where they are, I know where they are, I know where they are

If you want to find the old battalion, I know where they are,

They're hanging on the old barbed wire,

I've seen 'em, I've seen 'em, hanging on the old barbed wire.

I've seen 'em, hanging on the old barbed wire.

20

IT WAS STILL DARK WHEN I AWOKE, BUT THE CROWING of a cock told me sunrise wasn't far off. Wolf's arm lay across me and his head rested on my tummy. In between the fowl's calls, I could hear Wolf's slow breathing. Every time he exhaled, his breath tickled the exposed skin around my navel. It was hard not to give way to a small smile.

In the peace of the morning, it was hard to believe the previous day had been so chaotic. I thought of Junior. Why wouldn't he look at me? Why didn't he come see me? I rubbed my temples. I was thirsty and there was a bottle sitting temptingly on my bedside cupboard, just out of my reach. Not wanting to wake Wolf, I let it be.

He was my silver lining. I must confess; a part of me felt joy when his father asked him not to return. The blizzard of the past few days would be worth it if I could find a way to keep him ensconced in the protective womb of my love forever. If I could, maybe even the entirety of my miserable life would be worth it.

Junior just needed to marry me and take us away.

My thoughts were interrupted by someone banging on my door. I carefully slid out from beneath Wolf, hoping it was Junior.

It was Mr. Ofori. My heart started to race.

"Where's my son?" he growled.

"The son you whipped like a dog and told never to return to your house?"

"Whatever I do with him is my business. Where is he?"

"He's safe and he's happy."

He grabbed hold of my wrist. "Look, young lady—"

"I'm here, Daddy," said Wolf.

Mr. Ofori let go of my wrist, and I turned to find Wolf standing behind me.

"I'm going to give you one final chance, so come on, let's go. Today is a big day," his father said.

He looked at his father and then at me and then at the floor. "Yes, Daddy." He stepped past me.

Mr. Ofori's lips curled into a nasty, triumphant grin. "As you can see, blood is thicker than water. Go and give birth to your own."

"Goodbye, Desire," said Wolf as his father shepherded him off my porch.

I watched them go. I told myself he wasn't my child. I told myself that he was just being obedient, a good boy. I told myself he would have preferred me. But I couldn't stop my heart from stinging with an all too familiar emotion.

I looked back at my empty house. Wolf once told me that resonance was when a vibrating system set off greater vibrations in another system. That's what the empty house did to my heart. I started to walk.

My father always made us have breakfast together as a family. No matter what our individual schedules were, we had to eat the first meal of the day together. Teenage me saw it as corny and bothersome. "One day you'll miss it," said my father.

I sniffed and threw my head back, blinking back the tears. He was always right and I was always so stupid.

The sun rose higher. Soon I started to sweat.

Just as I had decided to return to my empty nest, a black Range Rover pulled up beside me. The tinted windows began to lower.

"Desire, baby!"

"Jeff? What are you doing here?"

"I'm coming to see you," he said, taking off his shades and grinning widely at me. "You haven't changed at all. Get in."

I climbed into the refreshingly cool air and shut the door.

He folded the shades and stuck them in the side pocket of his dark blue suit. "I didn't know where your house was. I have been roaming around for almost an hour."

I smiled. "So when you stopped, you were coming to ask for directions, eh? And then you saw it was me."

"Oh no. I knew it was you. Can anyone miss this your structure?"

"Silly boy," I said, punching his arm. I was actually glad to see him, someone I knew and who knew me.

"Well, my house is back up the road," I said. "You can make a U-turn here and then when we get to where that huge cotton tree is, we'll turn left into West End Ridge."

He swung the car around but sped past the junction.

"Oh, you missed it," I said.

"Let's get a drink," he said. "I saw a place."

The place he saw was a nice bar at the STC yard. We got a table under the open-air canopy.

"What will you have?" he asked. "They've got a bottle of Gamay back there."

"Fruit juice will be good for me."

"I'll have stout," he said to the waiter.

"It's been so long," he said, leaning back in his seat. "Let me look at you well."

"You haven't been in Ghana for how many years now? Like five?"

"Seven, actually. Seven good years out of this rubbish country. Nothing much has changed, you know? I thought when I returned, some progress would have been made, but nothing has changed. The roads are even worse now."

I laughed. "I'm surprised you expected something different."

"It's a shame." He shook his head. "So I hear you teach here."

"Yeah."

"And how is it?"

I shrugged. "It's okay. But it looks like it won't work out. I might have to leave this place soon."

"You should. What is in this town koraa?"

"What about you?"

"I'm still with Burnett & Huntleigh," he said. "I'm a division manager now."

"Wow. That's good for you. It must pay well."

"Yes, but you know I never was in it for the money. It's not like I need it."

"You these d-bee children of ministers," I said with a laugh.

He laughed too. He picked up a bottle cap that had been left on the table and rolled it between his fingers. "You know—"

The waiter set the drinks down on the table.

I pulled my glass of juice closer to me. The waiter offered me a bunch of straws, and I pulled one out. After opening Jeff's bottle, he went away.

"You know, I'm a changed man," he said.

"Really?"

"Yes. Back then, I was so caught up in my business and my work and vision for myself. But I thought about some of the things you said, and you were right. I never really saw who you were."

"Oh, I see."

"Back then I was stupid. I just wanted to have fun, you know. And you were fun. But you were more than that. And I couldn't see. But now I can."

I intentionally took a very long sip of my drink so I wouldn't have to respond.

"So I have come for you," he said.

Some of the juice threatened to make its way into my windpipe. "What?"

"Come on. If you jump in my Range right now, we'll leave all this nonsense behind. By next week we'll be in Dubai. I'll do some work, and by next month we can go back to the UK. You won't even have to come back to this godforsaken country anymore."

I just stared at him.

"I know when your father died you lost a lot of money and property, but a beautiful woman like you shouldn't be teaching in some useless town. With me, you'll never have to work ever again. I can give you everything a woman like you deserves. I will buy you anything your heart desires. You'll wear designer stuff, Gucci, Prada, couture, whatever. I'll spoil you like a queen."

"That sounds nice, but I don't think I can accept your offer, Jeffery," I said coolly.

"Why?"

"I've got my foot stuck in the door."

"What do you mean?"

"There's someone. I can't leave him. He matters to me."

"Really?" he asked with a sneer. "And who of your class could you have met over here? What does he have to offer you?"

I sighed. "Everything I so desperately need."

He sat back in his seat. "Look, I didn't want to bring it up, but I know what happened at your old job in Accra. Everybody knows and they say things about you, but me, I don't care. I mean, we all have our skeletons, right? I remember the things we used to do. And you know me myself I like that white powder. Sometimes koraa, I played away matches. But think about it, what decent job will you be able to get here? That thing with the student is the sort of thing that follows you around . . . "

The TV in the background caught my attention. A reporter was standing in front of the university auditorium interviewing a couple. The volume was low, but I managed to hear, ". . . going to be a historic day. This child is something special. We know he's going to get that perfect score and make everyone in this country proud."

Then it hit me, that day was the final!

Jeff touched my hand, bringing me back to reality. "So what do you say?"

I shook my head and rose from my seat. "Don't worry, Jeffery. I'll manage."

"Where are you going? Think about it oh. Like, really think about it. Will you get another man like me, a man who knows he's no better than you?"

"It's been nice seeing you again, Jeffery. Enjoy Dubai."

"I'm not going to chase after you like the last time," he called after me.

I just kept on walking and hailed a taxi from the roadside.

Jeff caught the car door as I attempted to shut it. "I have my pride, you know. You know me. I don't have time for you to play hard to get, if that's what you're doing. If you leave, that's it."

I pulled the door out of his grasp. "Okay, Jeff. Bye."

21

"THERE IS NOT A SPARE SEAT IN THE WHOLE auditorium, madam," said an usher.

I peeked behind him. The place was chock-full of people and banners and placards.

"Even the corners of the room are full of people," he said. "Like you should have come earlier."

I ran my hands through my braids and walked back down the steps from the auditorium doors. A loud cheer emanated from the room, causing me to pause for a moment and look back. I kicked myself mentally for being so wrapped up in my woes. A group of hawkers sat on a low wall under a neem tree. I joined them.

The one beside me was selling shirts with "Ayekoo Wolf-gang" emblazoned on the front.

"How much is one of these?" I asked him.

"For beautiful ladies, it is free," he replied with a toothy grin.

The shirt he pulled out of the stack was much bigger than me, so it easily slipped over my head. I tried giving him a five thousand cedi note but he refused to take it.

"You don't have a place to watch?" he asked me.

I shook my head. "I should have been here much earlier."

His smile got wider. "I can show you a place. Come with me. It's a good place paah."

He led me down the walkway running along the outside of the auditorium and through a crowd huddling beside the small windows. When we came to a wire fence with a small gate in it, he removed a small key.

"I keep the rest of the shirts back here," he explained as he fiddled with the rusty padlock.

Finally it swung open and we entered a small enclosure. He picked up a bench and set it down before a window. The window was positioned near the front of the auditorium and elevated, so I had a good view of both the stage and the crowd.

I thanked him and sat down.

Wolf stood in front of a flip board. His hands flew across the paper, from left to right, leaving step after step of the solution to an equation in his wake. His two colleagues stood on either side of him and attempted to look like they were contributing anything worthwhile.

Mr. Ofori and his wife were seated near the front of the audience. Mr. Ofori had his arms folded over his chest and his legs crossed, ankle over thigh. His wife was seated to his left. Much of her face was hidden behind a large pair of shades. Her head was tilted to the left and supported by her knuckles. Junior was to her left. He rested an arm on the back of his mother's seat. They all looked like they would much rather be anywhere else.

A bell went and the quizmaster, a short, bald man with a silly-looking red bowtie, cleared his throat and said, "Time's up, contestants. Let's see your work."

A pair of judges moved over to the opposing team's board first. It didn't take them long to shake their heads and mark them wrong. They then moved over to Lighthouse Academy's board. After a few seconds, they put a giant tick beside Wolf's solution. The entire hall erupted in a loud cheer. It was as if everyone in the hall was on Wolf's side.

"So at the end of round 2, Lighthouse Academy leads Central Montessori by 10,000 points to 4,500," declared the quizmaster to another enthusiastic cheer from the audience. When the audience finally quieted down, he added, "We will now move on to the third round after a short break."

I tapped the window frame to try and get Wolf's attention, but the jama chants drowned out my efforts. Wolf returned to his seat and stared at the crowd before him. I followed his gaze to his family. His father and mother seemed to be exchanging words. Junior leaned over and held his mother's arm. That seemed to calm her.

Round 3 soon began, and Wolf answered every single question himself with a fire in his eyes and voice that I had not seen or heard before. At the end of the round, the scoremaster announced the results: 15,000 to 8,500.

Wolf blazed a seemingly unstoppable trail towards the success he desired. At the end of round 4, the score was 20,000 to 11,500. At the end of round 5, it was 25,000 to 14,000. Lighthouse Academy had won. Wolf had won. None of his sheepish-looking teammates had to answer a single question in the march to victory.

Someone at the back of the room started to sing. "Sɛ w'ose wopɛ Wolfgang, w'ose wopɛ Wolfgang, Wolfgang na wo bɛ nya!"

Then the entire audience joined in. "YIEEE, YIEEE WOLF-GANG NA WO BƐ NYA!"

Even though I had my reservations before, I could not help but laugh and join in the standing ovation that followed.

Even the quizmaster joined in the applause. Then he said, "Congratulations to Lighthouse Academy on this wonderful performance. We are seeing something never before seen in all the twenty-seven years of this competition and that we may never see again. Seeing as victory has been assured, let us have a few words from the family of young Wolfgang before we start the final round. Let's welcome them to the stage with another round of applause."

His family rose and shuffled out of their row and into the aisle. Before they could start to move towards the stage, Mrs. Ofori looked up and in my direction. Our eyes met. Abruptly she turned and made her way towards the exit.

Both Mr. Ofori and Junior raised their heads and saw me, but only Junior went after her. Wolf's eyes followed her out as well. A few of the organizers approached Mr. Ofori with confusion written all over their faces. After a short discussion, they dispersed and Mr. Ofori climbed up onto the stage.

"Unfortunately, my wife and son could not be up here with me. There was a little emergency. I'll just go on. Certainly we are proud to be the parents of this amazing child, and we are proud our efforts to groom him have been successful. So I'd like to say well done to him, but the fight is not yet over. We are awaiting the ultimate prize. That's what we all came for."

"Ah yes, the ultimate prize," said the quizmaster. "A scholarship to an Ivy League school in the United States awaits our contestants if they can do the undoable, if they can achieve perfection. Thank you, Mr. Stanley Ofori."

Mr. Ofori nodded and returned to his seat.

"We are now beginning our final round. This is the challenging General Knowledge Round. Lighthouse Academy is now just ten questions away from an amazing feat. Already, the previous record for the highest score has been smashed. Already, they have won the competition. But will we see a perfect score? Let us find out."

The quizmaster picked up a card from his table. "Lighthouse Academy, your first question: 'While at Liliesleaf farm in Johannesburg, Nelson Mandela went by what alias?'"

Wolf stepped forward to the mic. "David Motsamayi."

"Correct for 500 points!" The quizmaster turned to Central Montessori. "Your question: 'Which country has the most pyramids?'"

The three students from Central Montessori huddled together in deliberation. Then one of them, a tall and skinny girl, came forward.

"Egypt?"

"Unfortunately, that is not correct. The answer is Sudan. Sudan has over two hundred pyramids."

The girl shrugged at her colleagues and returned to her seat while the audience cheered. I felt pity for her and her colleagues. The whole day was unashamedly about Wolf.

"Lighthouse Academy: 'During World War II, which English codebreaker created a machine to decrypt Nazi communications?'"

Again, without any hesitation, Wolf came to the mic. "Alan Turing."

"Correct for 500 points! Central Montessori: 'Musa I of Mali is more commonly known as?'"

This time, Central Montessori sent the only boy on the team forward. "Mansa Musa," he said.

"That is correct, Central Montessori. Five hundred points for you. Now for Lighthouse Academy: 'Who was the first wife of the English king Henry VIII?'"

Wolf strode to the mic. "Catherine of Aragon," he said.

"Correct for 500 points!" went the quizmaster, and the crowd cheered. "Seven more questions to go."

I was about to put my hands together when I heard a noise at the wire fence. It was Junior. "I saw you peeking through the window," he called out to me, and tried to push open the gate.

"It isn't locked," I replied. "Just unhook the padlock."

When he entered, I offered him a place on the bench. "It's been a while since we had the chance to—"

"I have something to say to you," he blurted out, standing.

"Okay. Go ahead, Junior."

"You're not who I thought you were."

"I never said I was anything apart from who I am."

"You lied that my father raped you."

"I wanted to protect Wolf. It was going to rip your family apart. I just couldn't do that to him."

He started to pace. "You should have thought about that before you started throwing accusations about! My mother saw you out here and she had to leave. She can't bear to be anywhere you are. Because of you, she's making noises about going to her mother's house. My parents could get a divorce. My dad could lose his position as HOD. You don't know the can of worms you have opened."

"Blame your father, not me. You talk as if I wanted it to happen."

He huffed and paused for a moment. "You know, you have to understand. My father isn't a block of wood. Sometimes it's like you ask for it."

My blood seemed to freeze in my veins. "What are you saying?"

"Some of the things you wear . . . "

"Oh my God."

"I'm not saying it's your fault. But who knows why he did it? You can be quite tempting sometimes. Maybe you made him lose control. Who knows? I just feel deceived. I thought you were different, special."

"Oh my God, Junior. I would never have expected this from you, never from you. Yes, I'm not a virgin. Yes, I have had many lovers. Yes, I have been promiscuous. Yes, I haven't made the best life choices ever. But are we tethered to our mistakes forever? Did you not say you loved me for who I was?"

"My father said you slept with one of your students."

I jumped up. "Hey, I never touched that boy. Yes, I loved him, I loved him so much. It was foolish of me, but he loved me, I thought he did, in a way no one did, and in a way I needed badly at the time. But I never ever touched the boy."

He shook his head. "I can't. I just can't. You aren't the person I thought you were. You aren't . . ."

"Oh, say it. I'm not pure. I'm Jezebel, right? Delilah maybe? Or would you prefer Circe?"

"So you think what you've done is okay and acceptable? You think it's good?"

"You're not even interested in why I did them."

"Your father died, I know."

"He didn't just die. The cancer, it metastasized to his bones. You don't know what—"

"Plenty people have lost parents! I lost my mother, and I didn't start sleeping around. Other people have been through worse things, and they didn't turn into prostitutes. Some things can be ignored. But this can't. I just can't spend my life with someone who isn't untouched."

"So you don't want me anymore? You're breaking up with me?"

"You did it. It's not my fault. You gave me no choice. I agonized over this for a long time. But you just gave me no other option. I can't deal with this. How will I feel touching you when I know God knows how many others have been there before?"

I wiped my eyes. "Okay, fine. I understand. You know what, Junior?"

"What?"

"Wolf was right about you. He was right."

Junior shook his head. "You and that boy. Becky was like that. I don't know why you let yourselves get caught up in his nonsense. He's a smart boy, but he doesn't understand anything, and you indulge him like he's some lesser god or something. What is wrong with you?"

I said nothing in reply.

"Aha, speaking of indulgence too, what's with you and alcohol? You drink too much. Don't you have self-control? I might as well tell you now. A lady shouldn't drink like that. Where do you even get the money to buy all that expensive wine? Aren't you struggling to pay your mother's rent? Apart from the ones lying about in your living room, there are like a dozen bottles hidden under your kitchen sink. I found them."

I still said nothing.

"That one koraa, eventually I would have made you stop." He put his hand over his eyes and rubbed them. "You don't even cook. Your house is such a mess. You don't clean. Since you came here, you've never been to church sef. Sometimes I don't get you. Sometimes it's like you forget that you're a woman. But trust me, I could have overlooked all that. I was willing to overlook all that because with time I could help you change. But having slept around and stuff, how can I change that? Maybe some guy will be able to handle that."

He began to back away.

"It's even my fault. I should have listened when they said women like you are only trouble. Maybe you'll find someone who will accept your lifestyle. Me deε, I can't. Goodbye."

I sat back down and tried to delay the flood. Nothing he said was new, of course. I always got my hopes up, only to be read the same old quotes from one of the ten bound volumes I had on the subject of my femininity. Some things were just not meant for people like me, it seemed. Being loved and wanted had its prerequisites, it seemed.

When I wiped the tears from my eyes, I found Wolf staring at me through the window. I tried to give him a smile and thumbs up, but another wave of emotion swept through me and forced tears down my cheeks.

"Lighthouse Academy: 'Who cut off the Dutch painter Vincent van Gogh's ear?'"

He kept on staring at me.

"No one from Lighthouse Academy? Wolfgang?"

Wolf finally rose and stepped forward to the mic. "He did. He cut off his own ear."

"Correct!"

The crowd erupted in its usual cheer and chants of Wolf's name. He returned to his seat and looked back at me.

While Central Montessori answered their question wrongly, I wondered if I should leave so my tears didn't distract him. There was nothing left for me here anyway. I could catch the evening bus back to Accra, back to my mother's lap and her I-told-you-so's.

"Okay, ladies and gentlemen, it's time for the final question. It's time for history to be made. Wolfgang Kwabena Ofori, step up to the mic for a place in history. I probably shouldn't say this, but this last question is a sure banker for someone as smart as you. But you have earned the respect of everyone here today, and we're proud of your amazing accomplishment, aren't we, ladies and gentlemen?"

The audience applauded enthusiastically.

"This is indeed a rare talent, ladies and gentlemen. So Wolfgang Kwabena Ofori, the question that will change your life is, 'What gland in the human body is commonly referred to as the master gland?' I'm sure most of us in the audience can answer this one."

Wolf did not move. He just stared at me, then his father and the empty seat beside him.

"Come on up, Wolfgang."

Wolf still didn't move.

"We're all waiting," said the quizmaster. "Your future is waiting."

Wolf just sat there.

People started to whisper. The quizmaster looked around.

"Imagine if he doesn't know the answer, talk about futility," he tried to joke. A few people laughed.

Wolf suddenly rose from his seat and approached the mic. The audience quietened.

He smiled. "You know, it's funny you should mention futility." He took the microphone of its stand. "I have a friend who wrote extensively about the subject. Let me tell you the words of my friend, the Teacher."

Panic gripped me. I knew what was coming.

"'I said to myself, "Look, I am wiser than any of the kings who ruled in Jerusalem before me. I have greater wisdom and knowledge than any of them." So I set out to learn everything from wisdom to madness and folly. But I learned firsthand that pursuing all this is like chasing the wind. The greater my wisdom, the greater my grief. To increase knowledge only increases sorrow.'"

I banged on the window frame. "No, no, Wolf! What are you doing?"

"'I thought, "Wisdom is better than foolishness, just as light is better than darkness. For the wise can see where they are going, but fools walk in the dark." Yet I saw that the wise and the foolish share the same fate. Both will die. So I said to myself, "Since I will end up the same as the fool, what's the value of all my wisdom? This is all so meaningless!" For the wise and the foolish both die. The wise will not be remembered any longer than the fool. In the days to come, both will be forgotten. So I came to hate life because everything done here under the sun is so troubling. Everything is meaningless— like chasing the wind.'"

"'So what do people get in this life for all their hard work and anxiety? Their days of labor are filled with pain and grief; even at night their minds cannot rest. It is all meaningless.

"'Again, I observed all the oppression that takes place under the sun. I saw the tears of the oppressed, with no one to comfort them. The oppressors have great power, and their victims are helpless. So I concluded that the dead are better off than the living. But most fortunate of all are those who are not yet born. For they have not seen all the evil that is done under the sun.'"

He wiped a solitary tear from his cheek and went on.

"'I have thought deeply about all that goes on here under the sun, where people have the power to hurt each other.'"

He wiped away another tear on his other cheek.

"'This, too, I carefully explored: Even though the actions of godly and wise people are in God's hands, no one knows whether God will show them favor.' 'It seems so wrong that everyone under the sun suffers the same fate. Already twisted by evil, people choose their own mad course, for they have no hope. There is nothing ahead but death anyway.'"

"'I have observed something else under the sun. The fastest runner doesn't always win the race, and the strongest warrior doesn't always win the battle. The wise sometimes go hungry, and the skillful are not necessarily wealthy. And those who are educated don't always lead successful lives. It is all decided by chance, by being in the right place at the right time. People can never predict when hard times might come. Like fish in a net or birds in a trap, people are caught by sudden tragedy.

"'For then the dust will return to the earth, and the spirit will return to God who gave it. "Everything is meaningless," says the Teacher, "completely meaningless."'"

The auditorium was deathly quiet. Some mouths were wide open. Some were covered with palms.

His eyes locked on mine.

"What have you done, Wolf?" I mouthed.

The quizmaster looked around as if for directions. Finding everyone equally confused, he said, "Erm, okay . . . so what is your answer?"

"Bɔɔla. Life is bɔɔla. That's my answer."

The quizmaster's shoulders sagged. "I'm afraid that is not the answer we want to hear."

22

THE ROOM WAS SILENT AT FIRST. THEN ALL AT ONCE IT
erupted into cacophony.

I watched from my window as the organizers spoke to Wolf,
one by one and then all together. His father forced his way onto
the stage and rained down expletives on him. His teammates put
a finger to their temples to ask him if he was insane.

Wolf sat there, arms folded and staring straight ahead.

After more than an hour, one of the organizers finally turned
to the quizmaster and shook his head. Wolf was then escorted
out of the auditorium. The cameramen orbited him, illuminating him with blinding flashes of light. Illuminating him so that
this his dark moment could be better preserved for the masses.
Better preserved so he could be better torn to shreds with
their self-righteous amazement and hypocritical indignation.
Already a man in the back had suggested a deliverance session
to a thunder-faced Mr. Ofori.

I tried to go down to the entrance, but the gate wouldn't
open. Junior had locked it on his way out. I banged on the wire

fence in frustration, but no one could hear. It was not until late afternoon that the hawker appeared.

"Ei madam!" he exclaimed. "You're still here?"

"Someone locked it," I said quietly, simmering.

"Oh, sorry wai," he said. "Let me open you."

When I got down to the entrance, the place was deserted. I tore off the corny "Ayekoo Wolfgang" shirt, threw it in a bin, and started down the steep road to the university campus. I put my hands to my mouth and exhaled onto them. They were shaking with rage. At the bottom of the descent was a roundabout. I turned right onto the road that led to Lighthouse Academy and further to West End Ridge.

"I bet this beats leaving the fencing team's equipment on the subway."

I turned. There was a large mango tree beside the road and under it was a large rock. Wolf sat on the rock. He smiled at me weakly.

In a flash I had my arms around him.

"I'm sorry, Desire," he said.

"Don't ever say that!" I hissed. "What are you sorry for?"

"I didn't get the record. I failed."

"You won the competition. You succeeded."

"If you say so."

I joined him on the rock. "Where's your father?"

"He left."

"What?"

"He was pretty angry with me. I guess I need to be taught a lesson."

"Oh."

"That was my last chance. I don't know why I did that. I just felt . . . I just . . . "

His lips started to quiver. He covered them with the back of his hand.

"Hey, it's okay." I put an arm around him.

That's when the floodgates opened. His tears poured like a river onto my lap, seeping through my jeans. I rubbed his head and patted his back. I myself may have been moved to tears if I wasn't glad he was letting all the pain out.

Gradually the river ran dry and the heaving of his chest subsided and was replaced by hiccups.

"It's fine," I said to him. "Everything will be fine."

He shook his head without raising it. "I've failed," he mumbled.

"Don't say that, Wolf."

"I'm a failure."

"Stop it, Wolf."

He raised his head from my lap and jumped off the rock. "I'm stupid. I'm a stupid, dense, idiotic, useless failure." He kicked the rock with every adjective he mentioned.

"No, Wolf. Come here." I grabbed his arm and pulled him close to me.

"You don't understand," he said. "I tried. I never used to have to try for anything. I knew everything. I could do everything. But now I'm slipping and I don't know why. I can't fix things anymore. They fight and they argue. I know if I can just be better, I can fix it and they won't fight and they will be happy." He looked directly into my eyes. "But I've blown it. I've blown it big time. I've destroyed this one like how I destroyed the first marriage. That's all I do, just ruin everything."

"It doesn't matter," I said to him.

"I wish that they would just understand that I try. I try hard, you know. I push myself. I know the names of Jupiter's moons. Venus's clouds are made up of sulfur dioxide, which is why it's so bright in the sky. Water has such a high boiling point because of intermolecular hydrogen bonds. Oxygen is so electron-greedy that it winds up being partially negative, making the hydrogen atoms partially positive. The partially positive hydrogen atom is attracted to a partially negative oxygen atom in another molecule, you see. I know why the sky is blue. I know why we can still feel the sun's heat even though there's a 149 million kilometer vacuum between us. You see, it's not that I want to be a failure. I wish they would understand."

I opened my mouth but he said, "Listen, I have many things in my head. I've seen it all. I've had to see it all. I have seen babies snatched from their mother's hands by great firestorms in Dresden. I know what happened in Nanking. I know about the Khmer Rouge. I know about Rwanda. I know about the *Hindenburg*. They burnt, Desire. The people oxidized with a release of carbon dioxide and water. I have feelings. They think I have no heart. But I *feel*. I've felt the pain, the pain of despair and loss, multiplied thousands upon thousands of times. In Nigeria, people go to the villages and they lure needy girls away from their homes, take them across the Sahara, they rape and impregnate them, addict them to cocaine, and sell them as sex slaves to clients in Europe. In Japan, a seventeen-year-old girl was abducted and tortured and murdered by four boys. They beat her, raped her, starved her, forced her to drink her own urine, burned her with cigarettes, inserted foreign objects into her orifices, dropped dumbbells on her stomach, dripped hot candle wax on her face, burned her eyelids, stabbed her, and cut off her left nipple. She begged for death so many times. Finally they set her on fire. I have this in my head." He tapped his temple.

"This knowledge hurts. You don't think I feel it? Why do humans do this to each other? I've seen the bodies, they were just hanging on the barbed wire. See Kutcher's *The Definitive History of the War to End All Wars*, page 165. I see the image every night. Those where people. They had dreams and love and hope. Do you know Vivien Leigh? Do you know who she was? Do you know what she sacrificed, the hard work she put in? She gave everything to her art, she created such beauty and wonder. Then she died. Blood filled her lungs. She drowned in her own lifeblood. No mercy was shown her. The universe gave her no pass for being special and dedicated. I have all this in my head. I have all their pain in my head. The price of knowledge is high. I do this all for humans who don't love me. They say I'm weird. They say I have a demon. Because I don't have feelings, right? Because I'm just a walking bookcase or a place, a receptacle, to put all their pain. That's my worth? That's all I will ever be? Why don't humans see that I have feelings too? I do everything for them, but I'm not loved. And yet people like that useless Junior have all the love. I ought to be their Adam: but I am rather the fallen angel, whom they drive from joy for no misdeed. Everywhere I see bliss, from which I alone am irrevocably excluded."

"I love you, do I not?" I asked him.

He looked back at me with his sad, old eyes. "You are going to die," he said. "First you will suffer, and then you and your love for me will die. As will I. It's coming for us all, the inescapable cold equilibrium time brings. I have seen it."

He fell silent, hands on hips and face to the ground, contemplating something. Then he said, "Anyone happy in this world is either evil, insane, or not very bright. But you're intelligent, how did you possibly make it to your age? Why haven't you drunk a disinfectant? I've seen what happens to the ducks when the lake freezes over. What have you done with the anger and the, erm"—he whispered his last two words—"the despair."

"Wolf, all these things you have seen in your future, the end of the world and stuff, have they happened?"

"No. Not yet, but they—"

"There's your answer."

"But bad things have happened to you. And you're still here. And you laugh and smile—from time to time."

"I guess my secret is that I just never learn." I laughed.

He laughed along with me. "So the secret to being a kind of happy, seemingly well-adjusted person who cries into their pillow at 3 a.m., is to just never learn? Just close your eyes and ignore the flashing lights and sirens in the distance?"

I smiled. "Let me tell you something, Wolf. When I was twenty-two, I had just started my master's program and I had a handful of stories published in several anthologies. Then one day my father returned from hospital with news. He had prostate cancer and nothing could be done about it."

"So what did you do?"

"I got pregnant."

He froze, smiled for a moment, and then chuckled. "What?"

I laughed. "Yes, it doesn't make sense, does it? But that's what I did. I sat on my bed and punched holes in my boyfriend's condoms. Also, I dropped out of the master's program."

"You're insane, completely insane," he said, smiling. "So where is he or she?"

"He. He was stillborn."

"Oh."

"So I understand, Wolf. I know what it's like to go completely haywire when you're caught in the headlights. And often I wonder what could have been and how my life could have been different. But what matters is how we respond. I don't want you to end up sad like me."

He nodded slowly. Then he asked, "Junior won't be marrying you anymore?"

I shook my head. "Apparently I'm not pure. And I drink. And I don't go to church. And I don't clean. And I don't cook. But most importantly, I'm not pure."

"I'm sorry," he said. "I really am."

"Don't worry. It's fine."

"It's not fine. I saw you crying when Junior left. And look what my father did to you. I don't get why you're taking it so well."

"I'll be fine. This isn't the first time it has happened to me."
He looked at me, eyes wide open.
"I was fourteen. My uncle stayed with us for a while. He came to my room one night with a bottle of wine and only one glass. After pouring me several glasses, he lay down beside me and told me how beautiful I had become. Then he started to touch me."
"Herh! What did you do?"
"Nothing. I didn't tell anybody."
He put his palm over his mouth.
"I knew it was wrong, but I didn't know it was rape, rape. He wasn't some kwashe boy or area boy or something. He was Uncle Johnny. He was young and cool and charming. Everybody loved him. Plus, he had just graduated as an engineer. I guess I didn't want to ruin him. So I just tried not to think about it. And ... "
"And?"
"I was kind of confused. Because I responded. I had a response to it. You know what I mean?" I laughed and said, "I can't believe I'm saying this. But after the first few times, I kind of looked forward to him slipping into my room every other night."
"I would have killed him," he said with dark eyes.
"Of course, I was disgusted with myself. I knew very well that there was something very wrong with me. Even though as a child I had always been a bit, erm, indulgent, I was never quite the same again."
Wolf didn't say anything.
"Also, I dunno, I guess I was also kind of in love with the idea of excess."
He frowned. "How? Why?"
"Well, I wanted to be a writer, you know? When I was a little girl. And all the really great writers embraced immoderation.

Think about writers like Faulkner and Berryman and Wilde and Hemingway and Fitzgerald."

"Fitzgerald died of a heart attack at the ripe old age of forty-four," Wolf said. "That was after he lost all his money and destroyed his marriage and career. Hemingway shot himself with a rifle he described as his best friend. Berryman jumped off a bridge."

I smiled. "That's the part they don't tell you about when you sign up."

He nodded slowly.

"You must think I'm some kind of prostitute, huh?"

"No, not really."

I sighed. "Well, I feel like one."

"Desire, Lady Mensah."

"Huh?"

"Never mind. There were some noises about a fourteen-year-old boy."

I looked down and away from Wolf. "He was a good boy. He was innocent." I paused. My throat was tight. "It's criminal to take that away from someone."

"It's evil," Wolf said.

"I keep thinking about what you said the last time."

"What?"

"'Misery is not wine-soluble.'"

"I don't remember that."

"Well, I wish I had realized that then. I wished I had taken control of my life, of the present before it became set in the stone of the past. Forget about the past, Wolf. Forget about the future. Take control of the present."

I felt something land on my arm and I slapped it. The sun had now disappeared below the horizon.

"I think it's time to go home," I said. "The mosquitoes are out."

"One just bit me koraa."

Hand in hand, we started towards West End Ridge for the last time ever. I could not help feeling low.

When we turned onto the dirt road, I felt his grip on my hand tighten. "Want to know the truth?" he said.

"Sure."

"I didn't know the answer."

I laughed. "Really?"

He folded his arms and pouted.

"Wait, you're serious?"

"Of course I am! Is this a joking matter?"

"Wow, Wolf. I'm sorry. I'm just surprised because even I knew that one. It was kind of easy."

"Biology is a pseudoscience," he said, his nose wrinkled in contempt.

I put an arm on his shoulder. "Well, it doesn't matter. I love you still and indeed biology is, er . . . a kliner wisshen . . ."

He smiled. "*Kleine Wissenschaft.*"

When we got to his junction, I stopped and turned to number 4 with a heavy heart. "It's where you belong."

His face went blank, but before he could say anything, the entire neighborhood was plunged into darkness. "ECG again," he muttered. "I guess I'll see you later then."

"Wait."

"Uh-uh?"

"Are you scared?" I asked him. "To go back after everything?"

"No. I feel strangely confident." He looked up at the evening sky. By reflex, I followed his gaze to the large full moon hanging low and ominous in the sky.

"It's red," I said, fascinated. "I've never seen the moon so red before."

"It's a bad moon," he said. He started to whistle a tune.

"I have to tell you something, Wolf."

"What is it?"

"I'm leaving tomorrow. I'm going back to Accra."

He nodded and looked away. "Okay. Goodnight, then."

"Come," I said to him and hugged him.

He hugged me back.

23

THE POWER OUTAGE AND ME HAVING NO CANDLES meant I couldn't finish my packing. I tried calling my mother several times, but there was no answer. With nothing else to do, I lay my exhausted self down on the carpet with a bottle of wine nearby. There was much misery to wash away.

Clouds had gathered in the sky, but the air was still, hot and heavy. Even I who liked warmth had to take off my top and fan myself with a newspaper. After a while, I stripped down to my underwear.

I put Jerry to my lips and frowned. Instead of relief, it was full of bitterness and sorrow and decay. I emptied the bottle in the sink and returned to the carpet and cried.

Twenty-five years ago to the day, my father took eight-year-old me and my friends to the children's park. We spent the entire day playing on the seesaws and swings. I was still wide awake when my bedtime came.

"I'm not sleepy," I told my father as he carried me to my bedroom.

"You have school tomorrow. You need to sleep," he said. "I'll get you some warm milk. It will help."

"Don't worry, Pa. I'll just cry."

"Why?"

"I imagine no one loves me and then I cry. It helps me sleep."

He held me closer and rubbed my back. "No, don't do that, my child. You'll get headaches if you cry too much."

When he laid me down on my bed, he looked into my eyes and said. "I'm sorry."

"For what, Pa?"

"For all the headaches you'll get in life. Anytime you get a headache from crying, remember I'm so very sorry."

Before long I was asleep.

My sleep was full of uneasy dreams. I tossed and turned. I would wake briefly and then slumber some more. Reality and dreams alternated and blended together until I suddenly found myself wide awake with a strange feeling that something was amiss.

Fear kept me from getting to my feet, so I looked around. There was nothing to see in the complete darkness of the night. After listening to nothing but deafening silence for a while, I decided I was just paranoid and closed my eyes again.

"I'm here."

I leapt to my feet.

"It's me, Wolf. I'm right here on your sofa."

My heart was beating so fast that I had to sit back down or I might have passed out. "Wolf! You scared me." With the knowledge that he was there, I could now just make out his silhouette. "Don't do that again."

"I'm sorry."

"How did you get in here?"

"I learned how to pick locks, remember?"

"You could've knocked. I would have got the door."

"I didn't want to wake you," he said. "However, it couldn't wait until tomorrow either."

"What do you mean? What couldn't wait?"

"All is quiet along the Potomac, now and forever."

"Huh? Isn't that like a poem or something?"

He laughed softly. "Don't worry, you'll see soon."

"Wolf, what's going on?"

"There's a problem we're going to have to fix."

"What happened?"

"Come, let me show you," he said. His silhouette moved to my door and opened it.

"Wait!" I called.

I felt around and found a dress. I pulled it on and caught up with him.

"Why are you being so cryptic?" I asked him as we trudged over to his house.

The clouds were now a bit thinner, allowing some moonlight through. That allowed me to notice that his skin was glistening.

"Ah, Wolf. Are you wet? What's that on your—"

He stopped and turned to face me. The clouds parted fully and I gasped. He was covered head to toe in blood.

"Jesus! Wolf, what happened?"

"I took control of the present," he said.

24

MR. OFORI WAS IN THE MASTER BEDROOM. MRS. OFORI was in the room Junior and Wolf shared. Junior was in the living room. They all had the same expression of shock and panic frozen onto their faces.

"She was going to leave," Wolf said.

I ran outside and collapsed on all fours onto the driveway, retching violently. Their throats had been cut open. Blood was everywhere.

"Your reaction is normal. Don't worry," he said.

I looked up at him. "Oh my God. They are dead, Wolf. You killed them."

"I was caught in the headlights and I went haywire. I'm sure you understand."

"No, Wolf. No. No, I don't understand. This is wrong. This is sick."

"There's kerosene in the garage. It would be a good accelerant. It has a high flashpoint, and it's not as volatile as something like petrol, so the risk of an explosion is significantly lower."

More vomit spilled out of my mouth.

"Focus on how much you hate them. It will help."

I wiped my mouth. "I don't hate them, Wolf. What's wrong with you?"

"But my father raped you! Junior rejected you, and my mother thought you were a prostitute."

"Still, I didn't want them dead!"

He exhaled. "They didn't feel any pain, if that's what you're worried about. I used phenobarbital. So don't worry. I just need you to help me. Imagine what would happen to me if you don't. I'd be taken away—away from you." He squatted and put an arm on my shoulder. "Paris must burn."

Round three of my stomach contents threatened to come up, but I forced it back down and shivered.

"Let's get this blood off you," I said to him, wiping the sweat from my face. "I'll take you with me to Accra. But we have to hurry."

We went back in and I washed the blood off him. After that he changed into clean clothes.

He then went to the garage and returned with a can of kerosene. We splashed it all over the floor and walls of the master bedroom. When it was empty, he got another can. We did the other bedroom. With a third and fourth can, we did the living room and kitchen. I avoided looking at the corpses as we doused the place. I couldn't bear to see them stuck in their final gasp for air.

From the kitchen, we entered the garage. Wolf motioned for me to wait. He went back in and emerged from the kitchen with the gas cylinder. He placed it down in the middle of the garage.

"We need to make sure the house burns as thoroughly as possible."

I poured the fifth can over it. "Why do you have so many cans of kerosene?"

After that, we shut the garage door and I made a pool of kerosene at its base. He gave me a match and I lit it.

I held my breath.

"Cathy would be proud," he said. His eyes glinted in the firelight.

I dropped the match into the pool. There was an immediate and loud roar.

"Let's get out of here."

We hurried away from number 4 and down to the main road. There was a terrific bang and the sky turned bright orange for a moment before fading to a dull auburn.

"Like clockwork," Wolf said.

Not long after that, headlights illuminated us.

Wolf turned and waved at it.

"Wolf, no!" I exclaimed. I didn't want anyone to see us.

But the taxi had already stopped.

"Boss, we de go the STC yard," he told the driver.

As we got in, the driver asked, "Have you seen that?" He pointed to the glow in the horizon.

"I wonder what it could be," I said.

The STC yard, fortunately, was mostly empty, and only a sleepy-looking young man inhabited the ticket booth. I bought us tickets for the five-thirty bus.

We sat on the benches in the waiting room. Several fire trucks sped past, one after another. Each one made me jump higher than the last.

"Be calm," Wolf said. "We'll look suspicious."

I fanned myself with my purse and took a deep breath. I could still smell the kerosene. It made my stomach turn. All this made my stomach turn. "Why did you do it, Wolf?" I asked.

"She was going to leave."

"No. That's not why."

His nostrils flared. "Well, was I supposed to take it lying down? Wolves don't take things lying down. We make them pay."

"Take what lying down?"

"Everything! All the things they do to me. The way they treat me. It was the little things. There was just a never-ending sequence of little things. And little things matter. Little things hurt. They shun us, they do these hurtful things to us. You think those words don't hurt?"

"Why didn't you tell them how you feel?"

"What?" He laughed. "Tell them how I feel? Let them know they have hurt me? Over my dead body." He shifted in his seat. "Besides, who even cares about our pain? Of what importance is our pain? He must never have any pain. If he does, he's weak and useless. I am weak and useless, huh? I showed them."

"Hmm . . . Are you sure about that?"

"What else could I have done? There's no space in the narrative for our humanity, just our hunger, our anger and lust. You know, I thought the grass was greener on the feminine side, but . . . but look at how they treat you. Did we write our own DNA, Desire? Are we to blame for being defective?"

"Shush! Lower your voice."

He glanced around and continued in a whisper, "Look at Junior. You know Rebecca was carrying his child?" He nodded. "Yep. She was about a month along when she ended her life. And he stands there and claims you are not 'pure.'"

I raised a brow.

"Uh-uh. It appears no one is free. For us to become what is demanded of us, we must lose a part of us. We must be less than human." He shook his head sorrowfully and said, "It is too hard and too easy to be us."

Wolf sat back in his seat, his head bowed and his hands in his lap.

I threw my head back and closed my eyes.

"One day"—he cleared his throat—"one day, I walked up to my father. You know what I said to him? I said, 'Daddy, sometimes I feel like a rag.'"

I looked at Wolf. He kept his head down.

"He said I should stop being silly. He said it was crazy talk." He smiled wryly. "Crazy talk." Then he folded his arms and we said nothing more to each other.

When the bus entered the yard, we boarded as quickly as we could. We took the back seats. Once everything was set and the bus started to move, the knot in my stomach started to unravel and soon I dozed off, exhausted.

When my eyes opened again, the bus had stopped. A sign outside my window told me we were just about to enter Winneba. Wolf looked at me.

I raised my head to look out the windscreen. "It's just a traffic jam," I said to him.

We both exhaled.

After about an hour, we were still stuck in the slow-moving jam and everyone was starting to get restless, including the driver. He hailed a motorcycle rider coming in the opposite direction.

"Boss, you know what de happen for the front there? Traffic no for de this part of the road."

"Some police barrier de there," replied the rider.

"Hoh! Here too barrier? Sake of what? Dem just de wan claim money. These greedy people." He kissed his teeth.

Wolf and I looked at each other. He looked away.

"I guess this is where I tell you the mistake you've made," he said.

"What do you mean?"

He turned back to me. "You failed to know several things about arson."

I gave him a look to show I didn't understand.

"Using an accelerant is a sure way to get caught. It leaves so many telltale signs."

"Ah. But you suggested it."

"And your mistake was to go along with me. Caveat emptor, Desire."

"I don't get what you're trying to say."

"Let me tell you what happened," he said. "When you came here, you were a disgraced former teacher and a sex addict with a drinking problem. You tried to start afresh, but it didn't take you long to slip back into your former lifestyle. You used your body to land a job and a nice bungalow to live in. Seeing your stillborn son in me, you quickly became obsessed with me—in a way you've been guilty of before. When it was discovered that you got the job with sexual favors, you were suspended. By then your obsession with me had reached the level where you tried to seduce me with alcohol a few times. After my father got wise to who you were and your plans, you accused him of rape—an accusation you later retracted. Junior then withdrew his marriage proposal. Angered over the loss of your job and boyfriend, you came over one night and kidnapped me and set my house on fire hoping you could escape to Accra with me."

"What? That's nonsense. I don't get it."

"To be honest, I took advantage of you. I knew your fondness for me would blind you to common sense. But take some time and think about the matter. There's no way we are going to get away with it. Fire doesn't slit throats. Three bodies would be found, not four. You're missing. The taxi driver saw us. The guy at the ticket booth saw us. There's kerosene all over the remains of the house. We reek of the stuff. Besides, what were you going to do with me when we got to Accra, hide me in me your bedroom? Someone has to take the fall."

My mouth hung open.

"Unfortunately, humans love a good narrative. No wait, not a good narrative, a familiar and convenient one. So they will buy my story hook, line, and sinker. It's quite unfortunate that your past has to work against you like this. If we want to get all pedantic about it though, it's as much your fault as mine. It's not my fault you are unskilled in tatemae. And you did those things in your past. You may have been predisposed to do them based on genetics and your environment, but *you* did them. I'll just connect random dots to give the illusion of cause and effect—of a narrative. Don't look at me like that. We do it all the time. Everyone does it."

"So what is this? Some grand game of yours? Everything was orchestrated? So you just used me?"

"It may seem cruel. But I did this for you, and for us. Yes, for you and me. They hurt us, so I hurt them back. And now all of humanity will pay for what they do to us. But they can't pay if I'm put away."

I covered my mouth and leaned back.

"When we reach that police checkpoint, it's game over for you. So you must run. When we get to the filling station just ahead, get down and take another car. Go to Kumasi or go to the north. Just get as far away as you can. When we get to the checkpoint, I'll say you got in a taxi and went back to Cape Coast. I'll give them a fake license plate number. Just make sure you aren't caught. Please."

He took my hands. His eyes were pleading. "Promise me you won't be caught. I will avenge you, mark it somewhere. The world will burn at my hands. Mankind will regret the day I came into this world. I will make the 'existence of the species of man a condition precarious and full of terror.'"

I shook my head. "You are insane. How did I not see this?"

"No, don't say that. It hurts when people tell me that. You of all people can't tell me that. I'm just doing what I must. Forgive me if I seem callous or uncaring. I just need to suppress all emotion to remain rational, and remaining rational is crucial for our long-term goal. I will suffer later on. I'm taking revenge for you. I'm just doing what I must. How did the

Athenians put it? 'The strong do what they can and the weak suffer what they must.' This is what you and I must suffer for our weakness. Make no mistake, I will suffer too. I care about your well-being now. I feel your pain. I don't want to hurt you, but to hurt them I must."

I turned away from him and looked out the window. I poured the kerosene. I lit the match. I brought him here. My hands were as red as his. Tears blurred my vision.

"I'm sorry," he said.

The bus pulled into the filling station and we alighted. "Just five minutes," called the driver. "The traffic in front of us no be small thing koraa."

We entered the filling station mart and I picked up a can of potato chips. "In case you get hungry."

"Thank you. Don't you need that? We could share a bottle." He pointed his chin towards a bottle of wine sitting seductively on the shelf beside us. "That Merlot is some good stuff. It gives me a really warm feeling."

"Get behind me, Satan."

I paid the cashier with what turned out to be my last note.

"Where do you think you'll end up?" I asked him as we exited the mart.

The sun was up, but there was a chill in the air.

He raised a hand to shield his eyes. "Probably with Uncle Max in Accra. He's the closest family I have. He's cool, so I think I'll be happy there."

"Great."

"You should do something about that stain before it's too late," he said.

I looked down at myself and realized that I was wearing the polka-dotted dress.

The driver blew the horn twice. The five minutes were up.

"I guess this is where we part ways," Wolf said.

"Yes."

"I have grown quite fond of you."

"Me too."

"I can tell your feelings for me have cooled somewhat."

"Let me tell you one thing, Wolf."

"What?"

"Lone wolves are failures."

"Huh?"

"I may not know about arson, but I know this about wolves. They are pack animals. They take care of and depend on each other. Lone wolves have no territory of their own. They feed off carcasses to survive. They quickly become sick and weak and they wither and die. Lone wolves are failures. I just thought you should know."

His mouth opened and he touched his chin. "Oh."

He turned and started to walk away, still lost in thought.

Then he turned. "At least you'll have pity, you know. If anything, you'll have pity. What about me? I'm just another wolf, skulking around the periphery, cold, hungry, and tired, while the lambs rest in the bosom of the shepherd."

I said nothing.

"Who will bother to fix me?"

I said nothing.

He looked down at the ground. "Did I reject the bosom or did it reject me?"

Nothing.

"Have you ever asked a wolf whether it enjoyed being a predator?"

Still nothing.

"What else can you do when you are given claws?" He stretched out his palms. "See! They didn't give me hooves. What else can a wolf do? What else can we do with claws?"

Nothing.

Finally he began to tremble and tear up. "It's hard not be who you are—the thing you were made to be. It's not like I have a choice. I had no choice."

I just stared at him.

He stamped his foot and tears went flying off his cheeks. "Why won't you say something?"

I said absolutely nothing at all.

25

THE BUS LEFT AND A BMW ROLLED INTO THE STATION and stopped at the pump. Loud, bass-heavy rap music thudded through the closed and tinted windows. When the driver's window rolled down, a young man stuck his dreadlocked head out and whistled at the pump attendant. A chilly breeze blew the smell of alcohol and weed in my direction.

Two other guys emerged from the car and went over to the mart, holding their crotches to support their sagging shorts.

"Chale, make you guys no kyɛ oh. We for catch the resort by three," the one in the car called to his friends.

He looked around while his car was being refueled. His gaze inevitably fell on me.

I was beginning to shiver.

"Hey you, fine girl," he called in an accent that didn't sound at all authentic.

I didn't turn. I knew their type; their fathers were either big men or they were sakawa boys. And I knew exactly what they wanted.

I thought about everything that had happened. I thought about Mr. Addison. I thought about Mike and Uncle Johnny and Augustine and Wolf and his father and his mother. I thought about Junior and Jeff. Then I thought about me.

"Ɔdɔ!" called the devil again.

But boy, was I cold.

I turned and smiled.

"Hi!"